Santa Sleuth

by

Kathi Daley

This book is a work of fiction. Names, characters, places, and incidents either are products of the author's imagination or are used fictitiously. Any resemblance to actual events or locales or persons, living or dead, is entirely coincidental.

Version 1.0

A very special thanks to the gang who hangs out at Kathi Daley Books group page for sharing their Christmas memories when I needed a boost to get my mojo back. This book is dedicated to all of you

Bree Heron
Barbara Hawk
Joann Hunter
Dawn Frazier
Linda McDonald
Taryn Lee
Kathy Kirkland
Bonnie Littleton
Sharon Robinson Dixon
Robin Coxon
Lisa Morin
Sandy Swanger Bartles
Donna L. Walo-Clancy
Shelli King
Peg Halley
Martha Hawk
Deb Forbes
Karen Borowski
Risa Rispoli
Kathleen Costa
Karen White
Van Loving Melton
Kathy Dunn
Teri Fish
Michele Hayes
Megan Smith
Teresa Terrell Fender
Dana Barrentine

Michele Hayes
Sharon Frank
Chassity Biddix
Cindy Olmstead Russell
Linda Kuzminczuk
Stephanie Treadway Hobrock
Janel Flynn
Della Williamson
Joanne Kocourek
Donna Pittman Robinson
Pam Paison
Chrissy Marie Raney
Mari Hinton
Kristin Wolf
Mary Brown
Misty Garoutte Clarkson
Lynn Hogan
Jeannie Daniel
Laura S Reading
Sharon Forrest
Martie Peck
Pamela Dennis Petteway
Vikki Partlow-Anderegg
Suzanne Boyd
Peggy Hyndman
Ruth Nixon
Christy Maurer
Linda Murray
TJ Morris
Mary Reese Robinette
Vicki Gardner
Sherrylrae Wicker
Sheryl Hagan-Booth
Janet Strasemeier

Sandie Dunlap-Mumford
April Schilling
Bonnijean Marlow Marley
Elaine Klingbeil
Hester Regan
Annette Guerra
Margarita De Jesus
Carol Smith
Betty Jo English
Sue Pippins
K'Tee Bee
Candace Wolfenbarger Knight
Yvonne Gilbert
Louse Ann Laba
Rhonda J Gothier
Bar Bristol Wiesmann
Stacy Smith
Janet Rose
Wanda Philmon Downs
Suzanne Sarnowski Marzano
Shelli King
Brooke Bumgardner
Kim Templeton
Stacy Smith
Toni King
Pat Walker Pinkston
Debbie Studstill Cox Hiemstra
Barb Kolasky
Diane Blaser
Judy Liggett Weaver

I also want to thank the very talented Jessica Fischer for the cover art.

I so appreciate Bruce Curran, who is always ready and willing to answer my cyber questions.

And, of course, thanks to the readers and bloggers in my life, who make doing what I do possible.

Thank you to Randy Ladenheim-Gil for the editing.

Special thanks to Nancy Farris, Joanne Kocourek, Marie Rice, Pam Curran, Vivian Shane, Teresa Kander, Wanda Downs, Elaine Robinson, Kathleen Kaminski, and Janel Flynn for submitting recipes.

And finally I want to thank my sister Christy for always lending an ear and my husband Ken for allowing me time to write by taking care of everything else.

Books by Kathi Daley

Come for the murder, stay for the romance.

Zoe Donovan Cozy Mystery:

Halloween Hijinks
The Trouble With Turkeys
Christmas Crazy
Cupid's Curse
Big Bunny Bump-off
Beach Blanket Barbie
Maui Madness
Derby Divas
Haunted Hamlet
Turkeys, Tuxes, and Tabbies
Christmas Cozy
Alaskan Alliance
Matrimony Meltdown
Soul Surrender
Heavenly Honeymoon
Hopscotch Homicide
Ghostly Graveyard
Santa Sleuth
Shamrock Shenanigans – *January 2016*

Paradise Lake Cozy Mystery:

Pumpkins in Paradise
Snowmen in Paradise
Bikinis in Paradise
Christmas in Paradise
Puppies in Paradise
Halloween in Paradise

Whales and Tails Cozy Mystery:

Romeow and Juliet
The Mad Catter
Grimm's Furry Tail
Much Ado About Felines
Legend of Tabby Hollow
Cat of Christmas Past
A Tale of Two Tabbies – *February 2016*

Seacliff High Mystery:

The Secret
The Curse
The Relic
The Conspiracy
The Grudge – *December 2015*

Road to Christmas Romance:

Road to Christmas Past

Chapter 1

Saturday, December 12

There was absolutely no question in my mind; I was going to kill my best friend, Levi Denton, when I next saw him. I loved the guy like a brother, but it seemed that as of late he'd been flaking on his commitments, and this time his flakiness had directly affected me. When I caught up with the guy he was going to be deader than deadonia.

"We're ready for you," Ellie Davis, the third member of the Zoe, Levi, and Ellie best friend triad informed me.

"I look ridiculous."

"You look fine," Ellie assured me.

"Seriously?" I looked down at the *much* too big Santa suit I was wearing. "The pants are twice as long as my legs, the jacket hangs down to my shins, and the beard is way too long, not to mention scratchy. I look like a kid playing dress up."

"The kids aren't going to care that you're a teeny, tiny Santa. They just want to tell you their wish, take a photo, and get a free candy cane."

Oh, God, the photo. I hadn't stopped to consider the photo. Zoe Donovan-Zimmerman, midget Santa, was going to be immortalized in photo albums across Ashton Falls for generations to come.

"Isn't there anyone else who can do this?" I asked.

"Not really. Levi still isn't answering his cell, Ethan had to leave, Hazel is busy with the craft fair, and I'm still not totally over my cold, so I really shouldn't be getting up close and personal with toddlers."

Ellie sounded fine to me. Her brown eyes seemed bright and cheery, and the red rim around her nose that had been apparent earlier in the week was totally gone. I hadn't heard her cough or sneeze all day. If I had to guess she was just using the cold to avoid Santa duty.

"I'm afraid, my friend, that until Levi finally shows, the part of Santa is going to have to be played by you," Ellie added.

I wanted to argue, but I didn't. Ellie had taken over as chairperson for Hometown Christmas when my dad, who was supposed to be in charge of the event, decided to go to Switzerland with my mother, who wanted to visit her family, so I supposed I owed her on behalf of the Donovan family.

"Fine. Let's get this over with." I pulled up the legs of the giant pants I was wearing and headed toward the Santa booth that had been set up in the community center.

I looked around the large room. It was beginning to fill up, although I knew the crowds would be three times as large the next weekend. The bulk of the Hometown Christmas events would take place the following Friday through Sunday, but the Santa booth, as well as the craft fair, sleigh rides, and ice skating rink, were featured every weekend between Thanksgiving and Christmas.

"Why don't you go ahead and get started?" Ellie suggested. "I'm just going to run into the back to get the camera."

"Very well. But hurry." I adjusted the pillow Ellie had placed between my T-shirt and the Santa jacket after I sat down on the giant Santa chair. The chair, like the suit, had been designed to accommodate a fully grown man and not a child-size woman, which meant that my feet, once I sat back in the chair, didn't even touch the ground. I just hoped there weren't any kids in line who were bigger than me.

"Ho, ho, ho," I greeted the first toddler in the deepest voice I could muster.

The child began to cry.

"Don't cry," I said in a softer and gentler voice.

The child began to scream at the top of her lungs.

I looked helplessly at her mother, who picked up her hysterical daughter and plopped her in my lap.

"She just needs to get used to you," the girl's mother assured me. "Why don't you talk to her while I run over to the booth with the ornaments?"

"You're leaving?" I asked with a slight hint of hysteria in my voice.

"Just for a minute. I'll be back before you know it."

I wanted to argue with the woman, but she took off like a flash, leaving me with her still-crying child in my lap. Geez. How *did* I get myself into these situations?

"So what do you want for Christmas?" I asked the toddler in an attempt to gain her attention.

She cried louder.

"I feel your pain," I sympathized. This was even worse than I'd imagined. People were beginning to look at me like I was pinching the child or something. "Do you want some candy?"

The toddler tried to wriggle off my lap. I caught her at the last minute, just as she was about to fall head first onto the floor.

I had to be the worst Santa in the history of all Santas.

"Sorry that took so long." Ellie jogged up with the camera. "I couldn't find the film. We really do need to go digital next year." Ellie looked at the child in my lap and then looked around the room. "Where's the mother?"

"Shopping."

"She left her child with you while she went shopping?"

"She said she'd be back in a jiff, but it seems like it's been longer than a jiff. I don't suppose you'd like to take over?"

Ellie set down the camera and picked the screaming child up off my lap. She immediately stopped crying. "I'll go find the mother and return her daughter to her while you talk to the little girl who just walked up."

I let out a long breath of relief and then looked toward the mostly nonexistent line. There was only one child waiting at this point, but at least she was a little older and didn't appear to be afraid of teeny, tiny Santa.

"Ho, ho, ho," I said as the girl, who looked to be about five, approached.

"Are you the real Santa?" The girl looked at me with doubt on her face.

"No," I admitted. "I'm Santa's helper. Santa is very busy at this time of year so he needs others to help out."

"But you can get a message to the real Santa?"

"Absolutely."

The girl reached into the back pocket of her dirty jeans and pulled out a piece of paper.

"Is that your Christmas list?" I asked as she began to unfold it.

"I only want one thing for Christmas," the girl answered. "I want Santa to find Cupcake."

"Cupcake?"

The girl handed me the sheet of paper she was holding, which featured a photo of a dog about Charlie's size with long black fur.

"Me and Dad and Cupcake moved to Ashton Falls a week ago," the girl explained. "On our first night there was a storm and Cupcake was scared. She was barking and crying, so Dad put her out in the yard. He said he needed to get some sleep for his new job the next day and she was keeping him awake. There was a hole in the fence and Cupcake got out. I've looked and looked, but I can't find her. Dad says I need to accept that she's gone, but I can't do that. I love her. Since Mom died she's my best friend. Please tell Santa that all I want for Christmas is to have Cupcake back."

I felt like I was going to cry. The poor girl was seriously grieving. I really wanted to help her, but I wasn't sure if I'd have any more luck than she'd had finding her lost dog. Still, I intended to try.

"What's your name?" I asked.

"Tabitha McClellan."

"Well, Tabitha, as I said, Santa is really busy at this time of year, but I know someone who might be able to help you. Her name is Zoe Donovan and she works at the animal shelter in town. If you want to give me your phone number I'll have her call you."

The girl didn't look totally happy about my offer, but she wrote down her number all the same.

"Can I keep this photo?" I asked.

The girl hesitated.

"To show Santa."

"Oh. Okay. Please tell Santa that Cupcake is the most important thing to me. We have to find her."

"I'm sure he'll do his best."

If my first two customers were any indication it was going to be a long day. I'd only been at my post for ten minutes and I was already an emotional wreck. No wonder the real Santa ate so many cookies. I was seriously in need of a little comfort food myself right about then. I was pondering the option of taking a break when a boy who looked to be about ten or eleven plopped into my lap.

"Ho, ho, ho," I greeted him.

"Cut the crap," the boy shot back. "I know there isn't really a Santa, but if I want to get the items on my list I have to pretend to go along with the ruse in order to please my mom." The boy plastered on a fake smile and waved to a woman who was wearing a red sweatshirt with a Santa face on it.

"Ruse?"

"It means con or scam. Geez, get a dictionary."

"I know what it means," I defended myself. This kid I really did want to pinch. Shouldn't there be an age limit on visits to Santa?

"Fabulous. Now ask me what I want for Christmas and pretend we're having a friendly conversation."

"And what do you want for Christmas?" I hoped the kid would be quick because he had to weigh as much as I did.

"I made a list." The man-size child handed it to me. "After I have my photo taken my mom is going to come over and ask you for the list. I'm going to pretend that I don't know what she's doing and she's going to pretend I still believe all of this is real. It's the way we do things."

"Okay. Good to know."

The boy smiled for the camera, and then walked away. As he'd predicted, his mom came over and asked for the list, and the boy pretended not to notice. I thought the whole thing was nuts, but both the mom and her son looked happy, so who was I to judge?

I was about to fake a sneezing attack and head for the back room when the most adorable little girl walked over.

"Ho, ho, ho," I greeted her.

The girl, who was most likely around four or five, climbed up onto my lap. "I want some shoes," she informed me.

"Shoes?" I looked down at the girl's feet. She had on ratty tennis shoes that were soaking wet from the snow.

"My sister got new shoes, but all I got were her old ones. I want some shoes that are just mine."

"Your name is Marissa Noltie, right?"

"Yes, I'm Marissa." The girl smiled. "Santa really does know the name of every boy and girl."

"Yes, I suppose he does. I'll see what I can do about the shoes. Is there anything else you'd like?"

The girl looked hesitant. "Mama says we shouldn't be greedy, but I really want a doll. One with black hair like mine and brown eyes. I saw one at the mall in Bryton Lake. She was so beautiful. She had on a blue dress and black shoes."

"And she came with a little white dog."

The girl grinned. "You know the one?"

"I do. Santa can't promise anything, but I'll see what I can do."

Marissa hugged me. "Thank you, Santa. One of the girls in my class said you aren't real, but I knew you were."

I continued to talk to the various kids who visited the booth and took photos for another hour before Ellie decided it was time for a break. After putting out a *Feeding the Reindeer* sign I headed over to the other side of the room, where Alex Bremmerton, one of the three minors currently living with Zak and me, was collecting toys and nonperishable food items with her friend, Eve Lambert. The girls had decided to take it upon themselves to organize a Secret Santa project to provide Christmas gifts for Ashton Fall's less fortunate families.

"How's it going?" I asked.

"Really well." Alex smiled. "Your idea to ask for specific items was a good one. We asked the teachers at the elementary school to have their students write out lists to Santa as a class assignment. Then we picked out the lists that matched the families we had identified as needing a visit from Secret Santa and made up a master list that reflects the wishes of the kids we're collecting toys for. We posted it a few days ago and so far over three quarters of the items on the list have been donated. We hope to have all the toys and food items for the baskets by the end of next week so we can get everything wrapped in time to deliver the gifts on the twenty-third."

"I think it's so awesome that you girls are putting so much of your time into this project. You're going to make a lot of families who might not otherwise have had a Merry Christmas very happy."

Both girls grinned.

"You know that doll you have at the house with the black hair, a blue dress, and a little white dog?"

"Yeah." Alex nodded. "She was donated a couple of weeks ago."

"Is she already promised to anyone?" I asked.

"Not specifically. A lot of girls asked for dolls, so I was just going to give her to one of them."

"There's a little girl named Marissa Noltie who asked for that doll specifically. I'll talk to her mother, but I'm pretty sure she won't be able to buy such an expensive gift. I'd like to set the doll aside for her."

Alex made a note in her little notebook. "Okay."

"Marissa has an older sister as well as a younger brother. If the family isn't already on your list add them."

"I will."

"Oh, and Marissa needs some shoes as well. I'm not sure what size."

Alex began flipping through her notes. She bit her lip as she concentrated. "I think I have information on the family, but I don't see it now. I'll look when I get home."

"Okay, great. Did you ask Zak about the hams?"

"We did," Alex answered. "And he said he's happy to donate one for each basket. He's going to throw in gift cards for the grocery store as well, so that families can pick up what they might need for their Christmas dinners."

"And you're still good with driving us around to make the deliveries?" Eve asked me.

"I'm very much looking forward to it. I can help with the wrapping as well. In fact, maybe we should invite a few others over to help. I can make some snacks and we can have a wrapping party. Based on the number of toys currently occupying the blue bedroom, I think we're going to need all the help we can get."

"Let's do the wrapping party on Monday the twenty-first," Eve suggested. "We should have everything we need by then."

"Do we have enough wrapping paper?" I wondered.

"I think so, although I'm not sure how to deal with the larger items, like the bikes."

"Maybe we can just put a big bow on them. Have you girls called all the families to arrange for delivery? I would think that a lot of the moms would prefer the gifts be delivered when their kids aren't home so they can say they're from Santa."

"Alex and I are going to call everyone and set up a delivery window on the twenty-third," Eve informed me.

"Great. It looks like you girls are on top of everything. I'll get the word out about the wrapping party. In the meantime, I guess I should go find Ellie and ask her if she needs me to do another shift at the Santa booth. If you need a ride home later come and find me. I'm sure I'll be here most of the day."

I headed across the room to where Ellie was refilling the trays that held sugar cookies and other Christmas pastries. I told her about the wrapping party and she immediately said she'd be more than happy to help.

"Do you think we should go look for Levi?" I asked her as I bit into a sugar cookie shaped like a tree.

"I don't know. Maybe. I'm getting worried. He's been late fairly often lately and he definitely has something on his mind, but it isn't like him to flake entirely."

"Have you talked to him at all today?" I asked.

"No. We had an argument a few days ago and he's been staying at his place. I haven't seen him since Wednesday."

I guess that explained a lot.

"Trenton just walked in," I told Ellie. "I'll see if he'll take over as Santa and then I'll go see if I can find the person who's actually signed up to play the part. Chances are he just forgot."

Trenton Field was a local psychologist and a member of the events committee, along with eight other community members, including Ellie, Levi, and me.

"That sounds like a good plan."

"I should be back in plenty of time to give Alex a ride home, but in the event that she's ready to go before I return can you take her home?"

"I'll keep an eye on her until you get back. It looks like the Secret Santa project is a big success."

"I'm really proud of the girls. They set a goal and are working hard to meet it."

"Unlike some other people we know. If you catch up with Levi, you might remind him that he has shifts the entire weekend and that we're counting on him." The annoyance in Ellie's voice was evident.

"Don't worry," I assured Ellie. "I'll give him a piece of both our minds."

Chapter 2

Sunday, December 13

I could hear Christmas carols playing as I slowly woke from a dreamless sleep. The room was warm and I could feel Charlie's furry body next to mine. I smiled and allowed a feeling of comfort to wash over me for a split second before I remembered.

Oh, God. What have I done?

I heard Charlie whimper as he nuzzled his little face into my neck. I lifted my hand to my head and felt the bandage that covered the gash that had almost ended my life.

The room was dark as I slowly opened my eyes. Charlie was lying on the bed next to me and Zak was snoring softly from a chair next to the bed. As my eyes adjusted to the darkness, I could begin to make out the images around me. A small table to my right, an IV stand to my left. There was a machine with flashing lights that I assumed was keeping track of my vitals. I'd really hoped to find that the past twenty-four hours had been some sort of horrible dream and that I was actually at home, preparing for the upcoming holiday. I closed my eyes and reopened them only to find that I really was in the hospital, recovering from what could only be described as the worst day of my life.

"Zak," I whispered. My throat was dry and irritated and it hurt to speak.

Zak didn't hear me, but Charlie began wagging his tail. I smiled at him and he put his paw on my stomach as if to say hi before jumping off the bed and trotting over to where Zak was sleeping. He jumped up onto Zak's lap, which caused him to open his eyes.

"Zoe?" Zak got up from the chair and walked over to the bed. "I've been so worried. You took a pretty bad blow to the head. How are you feeling?"

"Water," I whispered.

Zak went into the adjoining bathroom and returned with a glass of water. He helped me to sit up so that I could take a drink. The water was crisp and cold and felt wonderful as it slid down my parched throat. I remembered the burning in my lungs as I'd tried to breath in spite of the thick smoke that had drained the life from me.

"Kelly?" I asked.

"She's still unconscious, but she's alive. I really should go get the nurse."

I reached out and grabbed Zak's hand. "Jason?"

Zak hesitated.

"He's dead, isn't he?"

"Yeah, he's dead," Zak confirmed.

He left to get a nurse or the doctor and I closed my eyes and let the reality of the situation wash over me. I'd acted rashly and now a man was dead and Ellie's business had burned to the ground. I didn't see how Ellie would ever forgive me and I couldn't begin to comprehend how I would ever be able to forgive myself.

I looked at the clock. It said 1:11. The fact that it was dark indicated that it was 1:11 a.m. I'd gone to the Beach Hut at around four p.m. the previous afternoon. Had I been unconscious all this time? I tried to wait for Zak to return with the doctor, but I must have gone back to sleep because when I next opened my eyes, the sun was up and Zak and Charlie were gone. Sheriff Salinger was sitting in the chair next to me.

"Where's Zak?" I asked.

"He took Charlie for a walk. He should be back soon."

"Are you here to arrest me?"

"Should I arrest you?"

"I honestly don't know." I squinted as the bright light in the room made the pounding in my head even worse than it already was.

Salinger poked his head out the door and called for the nurse. He must have waited outside while she checked my vitals, gave me some water and pain meds, and readjusted my pillow, but the moment she left he came back inside.

"Do you feel well enough to tell me what happened?" Salinger asked.

I took a deep breath. My head still hurt, but the burning in my throat was much better than it had been earlier. I couldn't remember everything, but I knew that I owed it to Kelly and Ellie to tell the sheriff what I did know.

"Levi was supposed to play Santa at the community center yesterday but he never showed," I began. "I volunteered to track him down. I was driving past Ellie's Beach Hut on my way to Levi's apartment when I noticed a truck that looked like the one belonging to Jason parked in front of the restaurant. I was already both worried about and annoyed with Levi, and when I saw Jason's truck I just got so mad."

Salinger looked confused already. I guess I couldn't blame him. I was sort of talking in circles. I took a sip of water and tried to gather my thoughts.

"You were worried about Levi and that made you angry at Jason?" Salinger asked.

"Yes. I mean no. Let me back up." I took another sip of my water. "Ellie's assistant, Kelly Arlington, was in a relationship with the dead man who I only know as Jason. I'm afraid Kelly and Jason got themselves into this destructive cycle where he would beat her up, she would break up with him, he would clean up his act and ask for forgiveness, they would get back together and things would be better for a while, and then he'd beat her up and the cycle would start all over again. I wanted to tell you," I assured the man who had become my friend in spite of the rocky start to our relationship. "I almost did the last time Kelly was beat up, but she begged me to let it go. She assured me that she was done with the guy once and for all and just wanted to get on with her life. I knew at the time that keeping her secret was the wrong thing to do; I just didn't realize how wrong."

"The guy hit her often?"

"Yeah." I sighed. "He really did. Ellie and I were both so happy every time it seemed like she had broken things off with him for good and were equally upset when she would go back to the guy after she'd promised us that she wouldn't. When I saw Jason's truck in front of the restaurant I guess I let my irritation with Levi manifest itself into rage toward Jason. By the way, did Levi ever show up?"

"I don't know," Salinger said. "No one has mentioned that he's missing."

"He probably just flaked on the Santa thing and was spending the afternoon with friends. I'll ask Zak when he gets back. He should know." I put my hand to my throat, which was beginning to hurt. Salinger poured me another glass of water, which helped quite a lot.

"Can you continue?" he asked.

I nodded my head that I could.

"So back to Jason and Kelly," Salinger prodded.

I took a deep breath and continued. "I decided to see what was going on, so I parked in the lot next to the wharf and went inside. When I poked my head in the door Kelly and Jason were arguing. The restaurant was closed—the Hut closes at three during the winter—so they were the only two on the premises. I'll admit there was a little voice in my head that warned me not to get involved, but I ignored it."

I felt a catch in my throat as the seriousness of that decision began to sink in.

"I should have realized that Jason had been drinking, and that confronting him was the wrong thing to do, but I was so angry I wasn't thinking straight. I told them that I planned to call you to tell you everything I knew about the situation. It was the wrong thing to say. Jason slapped Kelly and accused her of spreading rumors about him. She began to cry and swore she hadn't, but I knew too much and he realized she was lying. He continued to hit her, so I attacked him with all the force I could muster."

"And then?"

I frowned. "Actually, the whole thing is kind of a blur. I remember fighting with Jason and then everything went blank. I remember waking up to find a fire burning all around me and wondering how the fire got started. I looked around to try to get my bearings and saw Kelly lying near the flames. I remember summoning enough energy to pull her out of the building. I guess I must have passed out because the next thing I knew I woke up in the hospital."

"And Jason?"

I closed my eyes as I tried to call up an image. "I remember seeing him lying on the floor, but I also remember thinking he was already dead."

"Do you remember how he died?" Salinger asked.

"I'm not sure. Everything seems distorted and out of sequence." I squinted my eyes as I tried to focus my thoughts. "Blood. I remember seeing blood. A lot of it. I remember knowing Jason was already dead, so there was no reason to go back in for him. I remember being confused and wondering if I'd killed him. How did he die?"

"It looks like he might have been stabbed. By the time we recovered the body the fire had destroyed most of the evidence, but we did find a knife lying near him. The coroner hasn't declared a cause of death yet, but he did confirm that the man was dead before the fire got to him."

I grimaced at the thought of what Salinger meant by the fire *getting* to him.

"I must have done it. There was no one else there."

"What about Ms. Arlington?" Salinger asked.

I rubbed my head as I tried to remember. I felt like the answer to what had occurred was just beyond my ability to grasp it.

"Kelly was already passed out. I remember Jason hitting her and her falling to the floor just before everything went blank the first time. I don't remember stabbing Jason, but I must have. We were the only people in the building other than Kelly and I'm certain she was already unconscious when everything began to get fuzzy."

"Maybe she woke up after you blacked out."

I frowned. "Maybe. How can we know for sure?"

Salinger shifted in his chair. "Ms. Arlington is still unconscious, so asking her isn't an option at this point. I don't know who stabbed the man we found in the fire, if in fact he was even stabbed, but I feel like I know you well enough to realize that if you were the one who stabbed him, it must have been in self-defense or in defense of Ms. Arlington. I don't plan to arrest you right now. What I do plan to do is to try to figure this whole thing out before my boss takes it upon himself to make an arrest. If you think of anything at all call me."

"I will. And thank you for having more faith in me than I have in myself at the moment. How much time do you think we have?"

"My best guess is that we have until the end of the month. The county offices are getting ready to shut down for the Christmas holiday. I don't see the commissioner or the district attorney wanting to take on a new case until normal business hours resume after New Year's. If we don't have this figured out by then my gut feeling is that someone from the county will step in and hurry things along."

"That doesn't leave us a lot of time."

"No," Salinger agreed. "It doesn't."

"So what do you know so far?" I asked.

"Our victim's name is Jason Overland. He was thirty-six years old. He moved to Ashton Falls from Orlando, Florida, two years ago. While living in Florida he collected a string of misdemeanors, mostly alcohol-related assaults. After moving to town he worked construction for Tyson Gallagher for over a year. He was fired eight months ago and has worked a string of temp jobs since."

"Do you know why he was fired?" I asked.

"Mr. Gallagher stated that Overland had settled into a pattern of showing up to work drunk and fighting with his fellow employees. Gallagher also told me that during the first year of his employment the guy did a good job and seemed to get along with everyone. He's not sure what occurred to change the man's behavior, but he began drinking heavily, and the more he drank the more violent he became."

What Salinger was saying seemed to fit what little I knew about Jason from my prior conversations with Kelly.

"Did Tyson think any of the guys Jason fought with held a grudge against him?"

"He didn't know for certain, but he didn't think so. Overland was fired quite a while ago and Gallagher didn't seem to think that any of his guys stayed in contact with him, though he didn't know that for a fact. Gallagher is getting me the contact information for his employees and I plan to interview each of them individually."

I closed my eyes and listened to the beep-beep of the heart monitor. This whole thing seemed so surreal. I kept hoping to wake up to find it was all a dream, but I knew it wasn't.

"Do we have anything else to go on?" I hoped.

"'Fraid not. It looks like you and I are starting from scratch on this one."

Chapter 3

Wednesday, December 16

"I didn't expect to see you here today," Jeremy Fisher, my assistant at Zoe's Zoo, the wild and domestic animal rescue and rehabilitation shelter we run, said as I walked through the front door with Charlie on my heels.

"I'm feeling a lot better and I needed to get out of the house. Everyone has been coddling me since I've been home and I needed a break."

"You do look better," Jeremy commented.

I touched my hand to the bandage that still covered the cut on my head. "The headache is gone and I'm pretty much back to my old self except for this gash on my head. How do you think I'd look with bangs?"

Jeremy frowned.

"Yeah, that's what I thought. I just figured if I could cover it up everyone would stop babying me."

"Maybe a hat." Jeremy placed a Santa hat on my head, which covered my entire forehead.

"A hat it is. Thanks for the suggestion."

"Actually, I'm glad you're here. Mrs. Vine's kindergarten class is coming for a tour this morning. Tiffany is off this week and it really would be helpful to have someone cover the desk while I take the kids around."

"No problem. I'll be happy to. It's always so much fun when the kids from the elementary school come by. Be sure to show them the hibernating cubs and don't forget to mention the mountain lions we set free in the fall. Oh, and the raccoons are always a hit with the younger kids and don't forget the kittens. Everyone loves kittens."

"Do you want to do the tour?" Jeremy asked.

"No, you can do it. I just want to be sure the wild and domestic sides of the operation are covered equally. Oh, and be sure to talk about being a responsible pet owner by spaying or neutering your pet. I realize they're only five, but it's never too early to start educating Ashton Falls' future animal owners."

"Will do." Jeremy grinned.

"Do we have any new residents since I was in last week?"

"A litter of puppies," Jeremy answered. "Five-week-old golden retriever puppies."

"Five weeks? That's pretty young for the pups to be without their mama."

"I agree, but they can eat from a dish and I've been supplementing their meals with puppy formula. I had Scott take a look at them and he thinks they'll be fine." Scott Walden was our veterinarian.

"Why did the owner of the mama dog bring them in so early?" I asked.

"Her husband got a job in Kentucky and the family had to move without a lot of notice. The woman didn't want to drag a litter of puppies across the country."

I supposed that made sense. And five weeks wasn't that young. I was sure they'd be fine. If we could find homes willing to supplement the puppy food with formula we could begin adopting them out before Christmas.

"Why don't you call Matthew Baldwin?" I suggested. "I know his golden passed a month or so ago and he would be knowledgeable and responsible enough to take care of a five-week-old pup. And maybe Estella Greenwidth. Her dog Hilda passed away over the summer and when I spoke to her last she mentioned she was ready to open her home to a new pet. I'd like to get as many pups matched with humans before Christmas as we can. How many pups were dropped off?"

"Ten."

"Wow, ten is a lot, but I bet if we put our heads together we can come up with enough people who would be able to care for the little guys and gals. Maybe we can ask a few of our more responsible foster families to take a couple each until the pups get a little older. They really should be in homes at this point in their development."

"I'll start working on it. Maybe Wayne Dayton will take a few. He's usually willing to foster several at a time."

"Good idea. I'm planning to stop by to visit with Kelly this afternoon. Wayne works a few doors down from the apartment building where she lives, so I'll pop in and ask him."

"How is Kelly doing?" Jeremy asked.

"Much better. She's being released from the hospital today and I think her sister flew in to stay with her for a week or two," I answered.

"Has she been able to remember anything?"

"Not a thing. She doesn't even remember my being there. She told Salinger the last thing she remembers was Jason coming by to see if she wanted to go out for a drink. Of course the last thing he needed was another drink. My memory is fuzzy, but I do remember that he was totally drunk already when I arrived."

"It's so weird that neither of you can remember what happened."

I shrugged. "Kelly took a pretty hard blow to the head. I talked to Dr. Westlake and he said her memory might begin to return at some point, but then again it might not. As for my own memory, I'm beginning to get flashes of images. The problem is that I can't quite sort them out."

"What kind of flashes?" Jeremy asked.

"For one thing, I think I did see another person come into the restaurant before I blacked out. I can't see a face or even a clear image, but I keep having this flash of a tallish person; a man, I think."

"Maybe he's the killer."

"I hope so, and I hope I can remember what happened. I really don't want to spend the holidays in jail."

"Anything I can do, you just need to ask," Jeremy offered.

"Thanks. Knowing that you're holding down the fort here is a huge help."

Jeremy picked up a box of dog and cat toys that was sitting on the counter and began decorating the little tree he'd brought in for the Zoo's lobby. In addition to the tree, he'd strung lights around the door and windows and hung garlands accented with red bows around the front counter. The addition of the Christmas music in the background gave the shelter a festive feel that made me glad to be there. Not that our house wasn't decorated. Zak and the kids had been in decorating overdrive for days. But there was something about being at the Zoo that gave me a warm feeling whenever I was here.

"Have you talked to Ellie?" Jeremy asked as he hung a catnip mouse toward the top of the tree.

"Yeah. Every day. I feel this insatiable need to apologize over and over again. She's been so sweet. She doesn't even seem mad that her business was burned to the ground. She just keeps saying how glad she is that Kelly and I made it out in time."

"Buildings can be rebuilt," Jeremy reminded me.

I picked up some chew toys and began to add them to the tree. "That's what she keeps saying. Zak has assured me that he's going to cover any expenses Ellie's insurance doesn't, including loss of income, but I still feel so very, very bad."

"And you still can't remember how the fire started?"

I frowned. "No. It's all really odd. I was arguing with Jason. He hit Kelly, so I attacked him, and he tried to hit me. I think I was able to avoid him. I don't have any bruises that would be consistent with being hit with a fist, but he did hit me with something. I think a chair. The rest is really blurry. There's this gap between my fighting with him and my waking up with the fire all around me."

"Maybe Jason set the fire, or maybe the person who came in did."

"If there was another person on the premises I just need to figure out who that person was."

"I'm sure it will come back to you. In the meantime, if you need a sleuthing partner I'm in."

I smiled at Jeremy. "Thanks. I might take you up on that. Zak wants me to stay out of it, Levi has been acting withdrawn and secretive lately, and Ellie is pretty distracted with dealing with the insurance company. Two heads are always better than one."

"Did you ever find out why Levi didn't show up at the Santa booth on Saturday?" Jeremy asked.

"No. No one could get hold of him for the entire day, but he did come up to the hospital to see me on Sunday. Physically he looked fine, but based on the stress lines around his eyes and his overall appearance, I can tell he's seriously worried about something. I tried to get it out of him, but all he would say was that he was working through some stuff and needed his space."

Jeremy tied a red bow to the top of the tree. "I'm sure he'll work through whatever it is he needs to deal with."

"Yeah," I agreed. "I do feel bad for him, and I feel really bad for Ellie. She seems to be dealing okay, but she has to be on serious overload. I thought I'd try to spend some time with her this weekend. Maybe do the girlfriend thing."

"That sounds nice, and if you need anything at all just let me know."

"I will." I picked up the stack of mail that must have been dropped off just prior to my arrival. I was willing to bet there were several other equally large stacks on my desk. "I'll be in my office until the kids get here."

"I'll let you know when the bus arrives," Jeremy assured me.

I smiled when I noticed that Jeremy had set up a small tree and strung lights around the window in my office. He was the perfect manager for the Zoo. He was thorough and thoughtful and really seemed to care about each and every one of our animals as much as I did. My new role as a wife and surrogate mom didn't allow me as much time at the Zoo as I used to spend, but with Jeremy at the helm I knew I need never worry that things weren't being taken care of as they should be.

By the time the kindergarten class arrived I'd sorted through the mail and cleared the messages on my desk. Charlie was thrilled with all the attention he was receiving from the group of five-year-olds and decided to go on the tour with them and Jeremy. I pulled a tall stool up to the front counter and began jotting down a gift list. I had a lot more people to buy for this year and I'd barely begun my shopping.

Zak was tough. He didn't really need anything, but he somehow always managed to get me the perfect gift, so I was determined to find the perfect one for him as well. I'd already considered and rejected all the typical gifts such as clothes and electronics. If Zak needed something or even wanted something he bought it for himself. What in the world does one get for the man who already has everything?

Zak's ward, Pi, wanted new computer equipment, which Zak had promised to track down and purchase. In my opinion Pi already had more stuff than NASA, but he was a computer genius on track to partner up with Zak, and I knew that like my husband, technology couldn't begin to keep up with his skill level and knowledge base.

Alex wanted new clothes, for which I had been shopping for the past month. She was such a practical girl, who only requested items she actually needed, such as new winter boots and a new coat because she'd outgrown the warm clothes she'd worn last year. I'd purchased these items in addition to some fun new outfits I was certain Alex would love, but I really wanted to find something personal and special for the little girl who had won my heart.

Our third boarder, Scooter, wanted new skis and video games. Unlike Alex, who never asked for *anything*, Scooter had a tendency to ask for *everything.* I supposed in a way this made him the easiest to shop for.

I also needed to find gifts for my sister, Harper, as well as my parents. Harper was still a toddler, so there were any number of items that would be perfect for the adorable child, but my parents were a bit tougher. I really wanted to buy my dad a new fishing boat, and I supposed I could actually afford it now, but I didn't want it to seem like I was being too extravagant after a lifetime of modest gifts purchased on a limited budget.

Zak had bought my grandpa a new fishing pole and I had found a fantastic patchwork quilt for his girlfriend, Hazel, at the local craft fair. I always get something for Levi and Ellie as well, but so far I had zero ideas this year. Maybe a romantic getaway for them, because Ellie was now unemployed and Levi had a week off every February for winter break. The way things were going, though, I wasn't sure they'd even be a couple in February. Maybe individual gifts would be a better idea.

"Is your name Zoe?" The same little girl I'd met when I was playing Santa asked after walking into my office. She must be with the school group.

"I am." I felt bad that in all the death and confusion I'd completely forgotten about poor Cupcake.

"I need you to find Cupcake. Santa said you could help."

"And I will help if I can. Can you tell me what happened?" I figured it was best not to let on that I was the Santa she had spoken to.

Tabitha explained about the storm and Cupcake getting away. "Can you find her?"

"I can't promise anything, but I'll try my very best."

Tabitha and I talked for a few more minutes. I located her house on the town map and we discussed whether or not Cupcake had a tendency to roam. She assured me that she always stayed in the yard, but the storm must have scared her. By the time we finished talking the tour was over and the chaperone from the school was instructing everyone to file onto the bus. Tabitha had given me her phone number and I'd promised to call her as soon as I had any news.

"Poor kid," Jeremy said after the bus pulled away.

"Yeah. It's not going to be easy to find the dog if she's been gone for over a week already, but I intend to try. I doubt she made it out of the area, but I suppose there's the possibility that someone from off the mountain saw her on the road and picked her up. Send her photo to all the shelters within a hundred miles and put an ad in the paper. I'm going to print up a stack of flyers and then head out to put them up in all the usual places. If Cupcake is out there we're going to find her."

"I want to find the dog as much as you do, but don't overdo it," Jeremy cautioned me.

"I won't," I promised, even though I suspected I would. Not only did I have a dog to find in order to make a little girl's Christmas wish come true but I had a murder to solve and a family holiday to prepare for.

"By the way, I wanted to invite you and Morgan to Christmas dinner." Morgan was Jeremy's daughter. "Zak is planning to make a big dinner and has been working on the menu for weeks."

"We'd love to come," Jeremy answered. "Although I suspect Phyllis might ask me as well."

Phyllis King was a surrogate grandma of sorts to Morgan and a good friend of Jeremy's. She was also the principal of the private academy Zak and I run.

"Zak invited Phyllis and the girls to our house," I informed Jeremy. "My parents and Harper will be back from Switzerland and are coming, as are my grandpa and Hazel. Ellie's mom is visiting an old friend this year and Levi doesn't really have any family in town, so they're coming, too."

"Sounds like a big group."

"At last count we have fifteen, but there's always room for more," I answered.

"It's a good thing you and Zak have a big house."

It really was. When Zak first bought the mansion down the beach from the boathouse where I'd been living, I thought he was crazy to buy such a huge house for one person, but it turned out he was filling it up nicely.

"Can I bring anything?" Jeremy added.

"No, just yourselves. Zak is insisting on taking care of everything."

Kelly called me just after noon to let me know she was home. I volunteered to pick up lunch for both of us and bring it over to her place. I had a few hours until I had to pick Scooter up from school and I figured there was no time like the present to really dig into the investigation of Jason's murder. If I didn't do it and Kelly didn't do it, I was determined to figure out who did.

"Burgers!" Kelly said when I arrived at her door. "I'm starving. All the hospital wanted to feed me was soft food."

I looked at Kelly's face, which was covered in ugly bruises. Her lower lip was still swollen, which I assumed was why she'd been offered only soft food. I remembered seeing Jason hitting her repeatedly, but it wasn't until I visited her in the hospital that I realized just how badly she had been hurt.

"I got them from the Burger Barn. There are fries as well."

"I like the hat."

"Jeremy gave it to me to cover up my bandage."

Kelly grimaced. I knew she felt bad about the way things had gone down. "Let's talk while we eat," she suggested. "You said you had some questions for me and I know you need to pick up Scooter from school, but I want to eat this delicious-smelling sandwich before it gets cold. I'm afraid the only beverage I have to offer is water."

"Water is perfect."

Kelly poured us each a glass of tap water and then joined me at the table. She cut her burger into small bites, making it easier to eat.

"So what do you want to know?" she asked.

I cut my own burger in half, took a small bite, chewed, and swallowed before I answered. "I know you said you don't remember what happened the night of the fire. I don't really either, although I've been having these flashbacks. I think someone else came in while I was arguing with Jason. I can't remember what the person looked like, but I'm almost certain someone was there. It occurred to me that maybe we should come up with a suspect list."

"A suspect list?"

"Yeah, a list of who might have wanted Jason dead."

Kelly chewed slowly while she appeared to be considering my question. "Jason wasn't a popular guy. He had a temper and he tended to make a lot of enemies. Still, even though he didn't have many friends, I can't think of anyone who would be angry enough at him to want to kill him."

I took a sip of my water before continuing. "That afternoon at the restaurant I noticed Jason was drunk. Do you know where he'd come from?"

"No, not for sure. He didn't say and I didn't ask. He used to like to drink at that bar out on the highway; the one near where they're building the new strip mall. I can't remember the name, but there's a big horseshoe on the sign."

"Lucky's?"

"That sounds right. I think he started going there when he worked a temp job out at the construction site. I'm not sure why he continued to hang out there—there are a lot of places closer to town—but it did seem to be his bar of choice."

Lucky's tended to attract a seedy crowd. I imagined Jason might have been kicked out of a few of the bars closer to town due to his propensity to become mean and belligerent when he drank.

"Do you know of anyone he hung out with?" I asked.

"No. He didn't like to talk about the things he did when we were apart. He considered his business to be his business."

I supposed it would be easy enough to head over to the bar to speak to the staff. Maybe Jason had met someone at the bar on the day of the murder. A friend or a colleague.

"Other than hanging out at the bar, what other types of things did Jason like to do?"

Kelly shrugged. "Nothing that I know of. When I first met him he was different. He was working construction for Tyson Gallagher and he seemed to have a close network of friends. He was up front about the fact that he'd had some problems in the past, but he seemed sincere when he told me he was trying to turn his life around, get a fresh start. Things were really good at first. He was kind and funny and we had a wonderful time together."

"So what changed?"

"He started going out with the guys. At first he'd just have a few beers, but then he began to drink more heavily and when he did, he got mean. Initially he was just verbally abusive, but then he started doing little things, like grabbing my arm or pushing me. I broke up with him a few times, but then he'd clean up his act and ask for another chance, and like a fool, I'd give it to him."

I finished my burger and wadded up the wrapper. I looked around for the trash can but didn't see one, so I just put the wrapper in the empty bag.

"When I first met you Jason had just recently lost his job."

"Yeah. He got fired. I'm not sure what happened. I thought Tyson was happy with his work, but I suppose he might have been causing trouble at work as well as at home. He was really mad about losing his job. At the time I was afraid he was going to do something to retaliate, but as far as I know he never did."

"Did Jason have any friends in the area who he might have socialized with in recent months?"

"There was a guy he used to mention. His name was Bill, or maybe it was Billy. I don't know his last name. I think they hung out sometimes."

I added *find out who Bill is* to the mental list of things to follow up on that I'd begun to make.

"I know you told me in the past that Jason had other temp jobs. Do you remember who with?"

"He worked cleanup on that big house they built down by the lake last summer, and I know he did a job hanging sheetrock for those apartments north of town."

I made a note of both. "Anything else?" I asked.

Kelly sat back, deep in thought. Then a strange look came over her face before she responded. "There is something." Kelly took a deep breath. "I think Jason might have been cheating on me. I could never prove it and he denied it when I asked him, but I got the feeling he had a thing going on with the tall redhead who works at that store in town that sells seasonal items."

"Tina Littleton?" I asked.

"I don't know. I never asked her name, but I noticed him noticing her more than once when we crossed paths, and when I went into the store to buy a Halloween costume, she got all flustered when I started a conversation with her while she checked me out."

Tina Littleton was the only tall redhead who worked at the store, so I figured it must be her.

"Do you think they might have been seeing each other while you were broken up this last time?"

"Maybe. I know he was seeing someone. He told me as much. He wanted to be sure I knew he could do just fine without me."

I frowned. "If he was seeing someone else why do you think he wanted to get back together with you?"

"I've been thinking about that a lot over the past few days and I've come to realize that my relationship with Jason was based on some sort of obsession on both our parts. We didn't really even like each other, but for some reason we both felt compelled to be together. My sister wants me to get counseling. After what's happened I think I might. I don't ever want to become involved in a relationship like I had with Jason again."

I looked at the clock. I needed to get going if I wasn't going to keep Scooter waiting.

"This gives me a starting place," I informed Kelly. "If you think of anything or anyone else please call me. I really want to figure out who did this. Not only did whoever started the fire kill Jason, they almost killed us."

"That thought has crossed my mind. My sister is going to stay with me for now, but she wants me to come home with her for good. I think I might. There really isn't a good reason for me to stay in Ashton Falls. My boyfriend is dead and I no longer have a job. I think a fresh start might be just the thing I need."

I hugged Kelly before I left. "If you do decide to move don't leave without saying good-bye."

"I won't. I'm not sure I even *can* leave yet. I imagine that until we get things figured out I'm still a suspect in Jason's murder. I imagine we both are."

Kelly was right. Finding Jason's killer wasn't just an option. One way or the other, I was going to track the son of a gun down.

I decided to stop off to talk to Wayne about fostering some of our puppies before I headed over to the elementary school to pick up Scooter. Ideally, we didn't like to adopt our pups to new families until they were eight weeks old unless we knew the adoptive parents well and were certain of their ability to care for a younger dog. Wayne didn't have any pets of his own, but more often than not his house was filled with dogs and cats that needed a short-term place to stay.

"Afternoon, Wayne," I greeted him as I entered the pharmacy.

"Zoe. How are you, dear? I'm glad to see you out and about."

"I'm doing better, thank you. I'm here to ask if you would have room to foster some five-week-old pups."

"As it happens, I have an empty house at the moment. What kind of pups are we talking about?"

"Golden retrievers. They'll need to have their meals supplemented with puppy formula for a week or two."

"I think I can handle four or five. Do you want me to stop by after I close for the day to pick them up?"

"That would be great. I'll call Jeremy to tell him to expect you. By the way, I wanted to thank you for coming by the hospital to check on me. Dr. Westlake told me you stopped in while I was sleeping and didn't want to wake me."

"When I heard what happened I wanted to be sure my favorite animal rescue worker was being well cared for."

I smiled.

"Shame about the Beach Hut. It was one of my favorite places to have lunch during the summer. Did you ever find out how the fire started?"

"Salinger is still looking into it, but he did say it appeared to be intentional," I told him. "He thinks whoever killed Jason started the fire to hide any evidence they may have left behind."

"That fire could have killed you, and Kelly too."

"Trust me, the thought has crossed my mind."

"I mentioned this to Salinger already, but I figure you're investigating, so I suppose I should mention it to you as well..." Wayne began.

"Mention what?"

"A man came in here on Saturday evening. He bought a bunch of salve and bandages. He said a buddy of his had burned his hand trying to add more lighter fluid to a simmering BBQ, but the whole thing seemed odd, considering it was snowing that day."

"Do you know the man's name?"

"No. He paid with cash and I hadn't heard about the incident at Ellie's yet, so although the BBQ thing seemed a bit odd, I really wasn't on high alert."

"Do you remember what he looked like?"

"Tall. About six two or so. Thin. Light-colored hair, from what I could see under the knit cap he was wearing."

"I'll ask Salinger about it. Thanks again for taking the puppies. I'll feel better when we can get them all into homes."

"Might ask Wiley. He was in a couple of days ago and mentioned that all the kittens he'd been fostering had been adopted, so I'm guessing he has room."

"Thanks; I'll do that."

Wiley Holt just happened to be a firefighter, and one of the first responders to the fire at Ellie's. Maybe I'd pick his brain about the fire while I was at it.

Chapter 4

"I'm going to be an elf," Scooter informed me the moment he climbed into the car outside the elementary school.

"An elf?" I asked as I waited for him to stow his backpack and get buckled up.

"In the school play. Jimmy Grogan was going to do it, but he got sick. I'm going to need a costume."

"But the play is on Friday and this is Wednesday. Aren't the parents making the costumes this year?"

"Miss Maxwell is going to e-mail you, but she said you can get a kit at the Christmas store. Can we go there now?"

I pulled out into traffic and headed toward the holiday store. I could kill two birds with one stone if Tina was working. Now that I had a list of people to interview I was anxious to get started. I just hoped the costume wasn't too complicated. I really didn't have time to learn to sew before Friday.

"I'm not very good with a needle and thread," I admitted as we headed toward the store.

"Maybe Ellie can make it," Scooter suggested. "Miss Maxwell said the pieces are all cut out; you just have to stitch them together. She said anyone could do it."

Maybe anyone who didn't happen to be me.

"So how was the rest of your day?" I asked as I veered onto Main Street. As it was every year, the entire length of the main drag that ran along the lakeshore was decked out with holiday lights, huge evergreen wreaths tied onto the lampposts with big red bows, and enchanted windows depicting a holiday theme.

"It was good. I got an A on my spelling test and Miss Maxwell put my science paper up on the bulletin board."

"That's wonderful. How did your speech about your favorite book go?"

"It was okay. I talked about a comic book and Miss Maxwell said the assignment was to talk about a *real* book we had read, but then I said that a comic book *was* a real book."

"Did she get mad?" I hoped not. Scooter had been doing so well this year.

"No. At least she didn't seem mad. The speeches were graded pass or fail and I passed. I really did know a lot of stuff about the story I read, even if it was a comic."

"That's good." I slowed as I made my way through town. "I'm so proud of how well you've been doing this year and I'm glad you had a good day."

"I did, and the best part of my day was that there are only two more days until break. Me and Tucker want to hang out. His mom has to work and he gets bored at his aunt's."

"I'm sure we can work that out," I said as I pulled up to the curb at the front of the store. "I spoke to Tucker's mom about him spending Christmas Day with us. His mom has a new job at the ski resort and has to work and his aunt is going to visit her husband's family. She's going to bring him by early on Christmas morning, so I thought we should get him some presents to open with the rest of us."

"Awesome. Can we get him a bike?"

"Does he need a bike?"

"He doesn't have one. His mom doesn't have a lot of money, so Tucker doesn't have a lot of stuff like I do."

I opened the car door and stepped out onto the street after instructing Scooter to step carefully onto the sidewalk. "How about if you and I go shopping this weekend and buy some things you think Tucker would like?"

"Video games. Tucker really wants video games."

It seemed all little boys wanted video games these days.

The Christmas store was as loud and crowded as it had been every other time I'd been there during the month. It was just nine days until Christmas, so you'd think everyone would already have all the decorations they needed. Of course there were decorating-obsessed individuals like Zak, who seemed to come home with a green bag with red lettering almost every night. It was a good thing we lived in a big house on a large piece of land; otherwise the quantity of decorations he had put up would be bordering on gaudy.

I looked around the large retail space. Ornaments, indoor lights, and fake trees were displayed to the left. Lawn décor, outdoor lights, and rooftop statues were to the right. In the center of the store was wrapping paper, boxes, and tabletop displays. I'd thought about getting a cute little Santa's village, but I wasn't certain we had any unadorned tabletops left.

Once I located the kit for Scooter's costume at the very back of the store I looked around for Tina. Luckily, she was shelving merchandise, which would make talking to her easier than if she was at the cash register.

"Why don't you run next door and get us both an ice cream?" I suggested to Scooter as I handed him a ten-dollar bill. "I'll take mine in a cup. I'll pay for this and meet you in the car. I left it unlocked."

"Okay." Scooter grinned. "Chocolate?"

"Always."

I watched him run out, then headed over to the aisle where I'd seen Tina. I'd need to talk fast because I doubted there was much of a line at the ice cream counter at this time of year and I didn't want to leave Scooter waiting out in the cold.

"Hey, Tina. Do you have a few minutes?" I asked as she stacked Santa towels on a shelf next to the reindeer hot pads.

Tina looked up at me and then glanced at the long line at the front of the store. "Do you want me to ring you up at the layaway counter?"

Even better. "Thanks. That would be helpful. I sent Scooter next door for ice cream and I don't want to keep him waiting."

"After all the money Zak has spent in the store buying decorations, I consider the Donovan-Zimmerman family to be our best customers. I'm happy to help out."

I smiled and followed Tina to the back of the store. I didn't think she'd been working at the seasonal store all that long. I wasn't sure she was even here at Halloween. Still, I had to admire her dedication to taking care of the retail outlet's customer base.

"I heard about what happened to Ellie's restaurant," Tina said, conveniently opening a dialogue that would lead to the questions I wanted to ask. Maybe my luck was finally turning around.

"It really is a tragedy. I guess you heard about Jason as well."

Tina's lips tightened. "I heard."

"Did the two of you know each other?"

"I hate to admit it, but I went out with the snake for a while."

I tried to sound as if this was news I was hearing for the first time. "I hadn't realized. I thought he dated Kelly Arlington."

Tina looked around the store after she slipped my purchase into a bag. She leaned forward and lowered her voice. "He did, but he told me that they broke up. He seemed nice at first, but it turned out the guy was a toad. He had a charming way about him until you got to know him and realized it was all a front."

"So you broke things off with him?" I asked.

"He broke up with me. Apparently, he met some floozy at Lucky's. He told me he was fine with sleeping with both of us, but Riley had a problem with it, so he was going to end things with me. I was pretty upset until I found out the dirtbag hadn't really broken things off with Kelly and was sleeping with all three of us. I swear, I've given up on meeting a nice guy in this hick town. I've pretty much decided to move home to LA after the first of the year."

I gave Tina a twenty-dollar bill and she handed me my change.

"Do you think he was still seeing this Riley when he was murdered?" I asked.

"I know he was. I saw them together at Lucky's on the day of the fire. I'm sorry Ellie's place burned down, but I'm not sorry someone killed the scumbag. He totally deserved everything he got."

"Do you know who might have been mad enough to kill him?"

Tina shrugged. "He used women like they were rags to use and discard. I imagine there were a lot of people mad enough to kill him, but my money is on Riley. I'm betting she found out he planned to get back together with Kelly and offed the guy. Based on what Jason and others have told me, she seems superpossessive."

"You know Riley?"

Tina shrugged. "Not really, but I did sort of begin to stalk her after Jason told me about her. I learned enough to realize she wasn't going to put up with some guy sleeping around. That chick is scary. I mean *really* scary. She looks exactly like the sort to stick a knife in some guy's back if he strayed."

I figured Scooter must be out in the car by then so I wrapped things up and headed out. It sounded like Tina had just given me the suspect I was looking for.

"Is this dog lost?" Scooter asked as I slid into the driver's seat. He was holding one of the flyers I'd printed of Cupcake.

"Yes, unfortunately she is," I answered as I accepted my ice cream cup. It was beginning to snow and I felt just a bit silly sitting in a parked car eating ice cream, but then again, I suppose it's always a good day for a frosty treat.

"Can you find her?"

"I'm going to try. I printed those flyers to put up around town. Do you want to help me when we're done with our ice cream?"

"Okay. It sucks that a dog is lost at Christmas. Are we going to put the picture in all the stores?"

"I thought we might. We're already parked on the east edge of town, so we'll take a stack and walk to the other end of Main Street. Do you have your gloves? It's getting pretty cold."

"In my backpack."

Scooter was an enthusiastic helper and we managed to distribute most of the flyers I'd printed before we returned to the car. We had a nice afternoon, stopping along the way to look at all the store windows that were decorated for the upcoming holiday and talking about plans for Hometown Christmas the following weekend. The only dark spot during our excursion was the sorrow that gripped my heart when we passed the charred structure that used to be Ellie's Beach Hut.

"How are you feeling?" Zak asked after we'd had dinner and were working to clean the kitchen after the kids had gone to do their homework. Spending this time with Zak as we worked together was one of my favorite times of the day.

"Okay. Tired and a little headachy but not bad, considering." I poured a small amount of water in each of the twelve poinsettias Zak had displayed along the window in the dining nook. They really did bring a festive feel to the house.

"Scooter told me that you stopped by Ellie's on the way home from town."

"Yeah. It seems he's going to be an elf in the play on Friday, and I wanted to ask her if she would sew his costume. She was happy to do it. She even said it would give her something to do, now that she had so much time on her hands. I can't tell you how bad that made me feel."

Zak stopped rinsing the dishes and turned to look at me. "It is not your fault the Hut burned down. Ellie doesn't blame you for what happened."

"Well, she should," I retorted as I returned the watering can to the cupboard where we kept it. "I may not have lit the match that torched the place, but if I hadn't confronted Jason none of this would have happened."

Zak didn't say anything, I imagined because he knew I had a point.

"You're going to investigate, aren't you?" he asked after he returned to loading the dishwasher.

I didn't answer. I knew he didn't want me to get involved in the investigation and I really didn't want to fight.

Zak poured soap into the machine and closed the door while I wiped off the counters.

"You know I would prefer that you leave this alone, but we both know you won't. I want you to promise me, though, that you won't do any investigating without me."

I turned and looked at him. He did look frightened, and I guess I understood that. I had almost died. I couldn't imagine how he must have felt when he heard I was in the hospital.

"Promise me," Zak insisted.

"I promise."

Zak let out a long breath. "Okay, why don't you tell me what you've dug up so far, and what your plan of action is."

I shared everything I'd learned, including the lead I'd gotten from Tina that afternoon about the woman named Riley, who Jason had been seen having a drink with prior to the incident at Ellie's.

"I was thinking about going over to Lucky's to ask around," I informed Zak. "Maybe someone knows where we can find this Riley, or someone might know something else that can help us. Kelly said Jason used to hang out there a lot."

Zak frowned. "Okay, but I'm going with you. The kids are all doing their homework. They'll be fine for a little while. And let me do the talking. You tend to get all fired up."

"Okay," I agreed. I was glad to have Zak's help with this one.

Lucky's was a seedy bar where beer and whiskey were the drinks of choice and everyone ignored the law in spite of the fact that there were "No Smoking" signs posted everywhere. Lucky's was a place for drinking and didn't serve food or provide live music. I didn't know it for a fact, but I'd heard it had more bar fights annually than all the other bars in town combined.

"It's so dark in here," I whispered to Zak as we walked in the front door. I coughed. "And smoky."

"This probably isn't good for your already smoke-damaged lungs. Maybe you should wait in the car."

"No. I want to stay here with you. Let's just make it fast and get out of here."

"There are two seats at the bar." Zak took my hand and led me across the floor. I really didn't understand why people would choose to frequent this place when there were much nicer bars in town.

The cushion on the stool I sat down on was torn and all I could think of were the germs that most likely lived in the exposed padding. I was glad I had on long pants.

"What can I get ya?" the bartender asked.

"Actually, we wanted to ask you a few questions," Zak responded.

"I talk to people who buy drinks," the man answered. "It's my job. If you don't buy a drink you aren't my customer and I don't have to talk to you. Now what'll you have?"

"White wine," I answered.

"Same," Zak added.

I was pretty sure I wasn't going to drink my wine. The place was filthy. I bet they didn't even wash their glasses properly.

The bartender poured us wine that came from a box. A very old-looking box. It was obvious very few patrons of this particular establishment ordered wine, white or otherwise.

"So what can I help you with?" the man asked after setting our drinks in front of us.

"We wanted to ask about Jason Overland," I began.

"What about him?"

"I guess you know he died in a fire on Saturday," I continued.

"Yeah. So?"

"I heard he was here prior to the event."

"Yeah. He was here," the bartender confirmed. "He was waiting in the parking lot when I showed up at two to open the place."

"Did he meet anyone?" I asked.

"A regular named Riley. They put down half a bottle of whiskey between them before he left."

"Before he left? He left alone?" I asked.

"Yeah, he left alone. I think they were fighting. I don't like to pry, but they didn't look happy."

I turned and glanced at Zak. I was supposed to let him do all the talking and so far I hadn't let him say a word.

"How long did Riley stay?" Zak asked.

"Most of the evening. I think she passed out at around midnight and one of the regulars took her home."

So she couldn't have killed Jason, I realized. Zak seemed to grasp that as well because he changed the direction of his questions.

"Do you know of anyone else Jason used to spend time with?" Zak asked. "Another woman? A friend?"

"Seems like you've used up the questions two glasses of wine will buy you.

I might be persuaded to answer a few more if you were to buy a couple of glasses of whiskey. The good stuff."

"Sure," Zak answered. "We'd love a whiskey."

We hadn't even touched the wine. Neither Zak nor I wanted the whiskey, but I guess that wasn't the point.

"So about that friend..." Zak said after he paid the man and left a generous tip.

"Jason was friends with a guy named Billy Sand."

"And where can we find this Billy Sand?" Zak asked.

The bartender eyed the wad of bills in Zak's hand. Zak gave him another twenty. Geez. Talk about extortion.

"Billy works construction next door at the mall. He's there most weekdays."

"Thank you for your time," Zak said before taking my hand and leading me out the door.

"That's it?" I asked. "He might have had more information."

"You were beginning to turn blue from lack of oxygen, and the group of guys sitting at the table behind us looked like they were planning to have you for their next meal. We've eliminated Riley as a suspect and we've got an identity to go with the name Kelly gave you. We did okay, and if we feel like we need more information from our friendly bartender we know where to find him."

I took a deep breath of the crisp, cool air. Zak was right. It was late and I was tired, and we'd done all right for our first day of sleuthing. I planned to check in with Salinger tomorrow for an update and then we'd take it from there.

Chapter 5

Friday, December 18

I sipped my coffee as the snow fell gently outside my kitchen window. It was early and the rest of the family wasn't up yet, but I found I couldn't sleep. Yesterday had been a long and frustrating day and I was beginning to think that finding out who'd killed Jason was going to be an impossible task.

I tried to take comfort in the warmth of the seasonally decorated room, including the white lights Zak had strung pretty much everywhere, the small tree in the corner near the kitchen nook, the fire that crackled in the brick fireplace, and the scent of bayberry candles that gave off a festive aroma. But all I could feel was a heaviness.

I got up from the barstool I was sitting on to pour myself another cup of coffee. I turned the sound system on low and selected a Christmas CD. The fact that Christmas was only a week away made me realize that I needed to get organized. There was shopping to complete, baking to do, gifts to wrap, cards to mail, Secret

Santa deliveries to make, and Hometown Christmas obligations to meet. I really didn't have time to chase after a killer, but the more I pondered the situation, the more I realized I would never find peace until I knew who had killed Jason.

I decided to mix up some cranberry nut muffins while I waited for the family join me. I'd already drunk three cups of coffee and it seemed prudent to eat food of some sort before I started on a fourth.

I'd begun my investigation the previous day by paying a visit to Salinger. He'd managed to track down and interview all the men Jason had worked with when he was doing construction for Tyson Gallagher. Everyone had reported the same thing: Jason started off as a good worker and a pleasant guy to hang out with after work, but his personality had changed as time went on until he'd pretty much driven a wedge between himself and every other man on the crew. Salinger reported that while none of the men had really liked him, they hadn't spent any time with him in the past eight months and therefore didn't appear to have a motive to kIll him.

After I spoke to Salinger I decided to try to track down Billy Sand. Zak didn't want me sleuthing alone, but he was tied up at the Academy that day so I asked Ellie to go with me. It was fun to have her as a partner once again.

Billy's answers to my questions seemed to mimic that of the men Salinger had spoken to. He'd started off friends, but things had gone south, and after Jason had totally blown the temp job Billy had gotten him at the construction site he'd cut him out of his life. He said he hadn't seen Jason in weeks.

The one result of my conversation with Billy was to wonder what it was Jason had been doing during the time he had been split up from Kelly. She said he hadn't wanted to talk about it, Billy said he hadn't seen him, Tina reported that he'd broken things off with her; in my mind, that just left Riley. If she'd been at the bar the entire evening of the fire she hadn't killed him, but maybe she knew what he had been doing. I decided I really needed to find a way to speak to her.

"What are you doing up so early?" Alex asked as she wandered into the room with Bella and all three cats on her heels. Charlie trotted over to say hi before the animals headed into the laundry room for their morning meal.

"Couldn't sleep. How about you?"

"Same."

"I'm making muffins. Do you want some hot cocoa to go with them?"

"Thanks, but I can make it." Alex headed over to the refrigerator for the milk.

"I can't believe it's only a week until Christmas. Are you getting excited?" I asked.

"Yeah, I guess." Alex poured milk into a pan, which she then set on a burner on the stove.

"You don't sound very excited," I observed.

"I am. I just have this assignment for one of my classes at the middle school that's due today and I'm still not finished with it. It's sort of stressing me out."

Alex began stirring chocolate into the warm milk. I had to admit I was surprised. Alex was an intelligent and conscientious student who rarely had difficulty with her assignments.

"What kind of assignment is it?" I was rarely able to help her with her homework, but it seemed important to ask.

"I'm supposed to write a paragraph about my favorite Christmas tradition and then share it with the class. The problem is that prior to last Christmas, when I came to visit you and Zak, I'd never had a traditional Christmas, so I don't really have any traditions."

"You could share something we did last year," I suggested as Scooter wandered into the room with his dog Digger following him.

"If you do something one time is it considered a tradition?" Alex asked.

"Sure. I don't see why not, if it was something you enjoyed and plan to do every year. What did we do last year that you want to do again this year?"

Alex sat quietly, I assumed to consider my question.

"When I was little, before my mom died," Scooter said, "me and Mom and Dad would all sleep on the floor in the living room on Christmas Eve. Mom would leave the tree lights on, and I can remember looking up at all those colorful lights as I went to sleep."

"That's nice." I smiled at Scooter. Sometimes I forgot that the all-but-orphaned little boy once was part of a warm and loving family.

"And when we got up in the morning all of our stockings were filled with candy and presents. After we opened presents Mom would make breakfast while Dad helped me put together whatever toys I got." Scooter got a sad look on his face. "I still remember the way Mom would smell like cinnamon from making her homemade rolls."

I wanted to pull Scooter into my arms and give him a hug, but I could tell he wouldn't welcome my affection at this moment. Better to pretend I hadn't noticed the look of longing on his face.

"One of the kids in my class told us that every person in his family gets to pick out a special ornament to put on the tree," Alex shared. "The whole family goes to the Christmas store and they each pick out what they want to hang on the tree that year, and then they drive around town and look at all the lights. After that they pick up a pizza and take it home and decorate the tree with the ornaments from that year and the ones from the past."

"I love that idea," I commented. "We've already decorated our tree this year, but maybe we can go into town this weekend and everyone can pick out one thing to add to it."

I slid the tray of muffins in the oven and set the timer.

"I'm going to get an ornament that looks like skis because I'm hoping to get new skis this year," Scooter said.

"What about you, Alex?" I asked. "What kind of an ornament do you want to get?"

"I'm not sure. I guess I'll have to look to see what they have. Scooter's new tradition sounds like fun, but I think my favorite thing from last year that I most want to do this year is go around and look at all the windows on Main."

"My dad took me to see the windows every year when I was a little girl and I've gone every year since I've been an adult," I informed Alex. "Maybe looking at the windows is a tradition we can share."

"While looking at the windows was my favorite thing from last year, I think doing the Secret Santa project is my favorite thing from this year. Eve and I have already talked about doing it again next year. Maybe I'll use that for my paper. I'll title it 'New Traditions.'"

"Sounds like a good idea."

"I want to go ice skating again," Scooter chimed in.

"I think we can do that as well. In fact, I planned for us to spend a good part of the weekend in town enjoying Hometown Christmas as a family." I just hoped sleuthing wouldn't get in the way.

"Can Eve and Pepper come with us?" Alex asked.

"I thought Pepper was going home for the holiday."

"I guess it isn't going to work out for her to go home after all." Prudence Pepperton—Pepper for short—was another of the three students living with Phyllis.

"Oh, no. What happened?" I asked.

"She was all set to go home when her dad called to say that he was taking his new family to Aspen for Christmas, so he felt it was best that she stayed in Ashton Falls."

Poor Pepper. Her mother had committed suicide after her father divorced her and moved on to a new family. Pepper had hoped to mend fences with her father in spite of the way he'd treated her mother, but it seemed he didn't mirror her desire to share their lives. The main reason Pepper was boarding with Phyllis and attending Zimmerman Academy this year was that her father wanted her out of his hair. I felt so bad for the poor girl who was having such a hard time with both her mother's death and her father's desertion.

"Eve and Pepper can absolutely go with us if they want to," I answered. "Brooklyn can come too."

Brooklyn Banks was the third student boarding with Phyllis.

"I think Brooklyn is going home for the holiday."

"Can Tucker come?" Scooter asked.

"Sure, why not? The more the merrier."

"The more the merrier what?" Zak asked as he wandered into the kitchen.

I explained about the weekend outing the kids and I were planning.

"Sounds like a lot of fun." Zak poured a cup of coffee. "My favorite part is the sleigh ride. We can't forget to do that."

"Do you have any traditions from when you were a kid?" Alex asked Zak.

Pi wandered in and joined us as Zak shared memories from his past. This, I realized, was the type of big family meal I'd dreamed of as a kid. I wasn't sure what the future held, or how long Pi, Alex, and Scooter would be with us, but I knew in my heart that I would always remember this breakfast.

I decided to stop by to visit with Ellie after I dropped Scooter off at school. I really did want to make plans to do something with her this weekend. I knew that between Scooter's play that evening and Hometown Christmas with the family time was going to be tight, but Ellie was my best friend and no matter what else I had going on I would make time for the person who had been there for me whenever I needed her over the years.

"Please tell me you aren't here to apologize again for the fire," Ellie greeted me when I knocked on her door.

"I'm not." Okay, I was, but I didn't need to say so. "I just wanted to see if you wanted to do something this weekend. Just the two of us."

Charlie greeted her dog, Shep, as we followed Ellie into the warmth of the boathouse. Ellie had decorated the small space warmly with just a few well-placed accents to bring the feel of the holiday into the home without making it feel crowded or cluttered. I loved living with Zak and I loved my new noisy family, but there were times when I missed the peace and serenity I'd found living in my own little space.

"I thought Scooter's play was tonight," Ellie pointed out.

"It is. And I have plans with the family tomorrow. Maybe Sunday?"

Ellie sighed. "Maybe."

"Something wrong?"

Ellie handed me a cup of coffee. I didn't want to admit I'd already had five cups that morning so I took a small sip and then set it down on the small dining table she'd tucked into the window nook.

"It's Levi. I'm pretty sure he wants to break things off between us."

I frowned. "Did he say as much?"

Ellie set a plate of Christmas cookies on the table.

"No, but he's been distant. Actually, more than distant. Downright evasive. I know something is going on, but whenever I ask him about it he just gives me some vague answer about needing to work things through. I think there might be someone else."

"I'm sure it's not that. Levi wouldn't cheat on you."

"Maybe not, but something is going on. And it's something he refuses to talk about, so all I've been able to come up with is that he has a thing going on with someone else."

I took a bite of my cookie. Ellie wasn't wrong about the fact that Levi had been distant and evasive, but another woman? I found that hard to believe.

"How is the investigation going?" Ellie asked. "Any news since we spoke to Billy yesterday?"

It seemed obvious that Ellie wanted to change the subject and suddenly so did I.

"I think we've pretty much hit a dead end. Between Salinger and me, we've eliminated all our suspects. There is one woman I still want to talk to, though. She goes by the name of Riley. For some reason I didn't think to get a last name. She was at Lucky's at the time of the fire, so she couldn't have done it, but it sounds like she might have been in a relationship of some sort with Jason, and I know she was with him just prior to his altercation with Kelly."

Ellie frowned. "That name sounds familiar."

"Tina Littleton indicated that she'd been sleeping with Jason at the same time she was."

"Tina Littleton was sleeping with Jason?"

"Apparently. From what I've been able to find out it seems the guy got around."

I realized that a discussion about cheating men wasn't the best topic after what Ellie had just told me.

"You know," Ellie said, "I think the woman who owns that motorcycle shop out on the highway is named Riley."

"You mean the one with the pink Harley hoisted up onto that platform a good two stories off the ground?"

"That's the one."

The shop Ellie was referring to was just outside of town. It didn't seem to me that Ashton Falls was large enough to support its own motorcycle dealer, but I knew the shop did repairs on motorcycles and domestic vehicles as well.

"Feel like doing the sleuthing thing with me again today?" I asked.

Ellie paused. "I still need to grab a shower. Will you wait?"

"Yeah," I agreed. "I'll take Shep out for a quick run while you get ready."

Shep took care of his morning business and Ellie got dressed, and then she, the dogs, and I headed toward the highway that led out of town.

Riley looked exactly like I thought she would. She was tall and thin with dark hair and so many tattoos covering her body that you could barely make out the original shade of her skin. She had long hair that was pulled back in a braid that nearly reached her waist and wore dark lipstick and eye liner that accentuated the piercings in her lip and eyebrow.

"Can I help you?" she asked as we walked into the shop.

"Are you Riley?" I asked, just to be certain the woman actually was the person I was looking for.

"Who wants to know?"

"My name is Zoe. I'm looking into Jason Overland's death."

"I know who you are. You're the animal shelter lady who's always nosing around in everyone's business."

"Yeah, I guess I am. Do you have a few minutes?"

Riley turned and walked down the hall. I looked at Ellie, who shrugged, and we followed her. The hallway opened up to a large room filled with partially disassembled vehicles and motorcycles. There were three men dressed in blue overalls working on the various vehicles. Based on the grease stains on Riley's hands, I was willing to bet she worked on the vehicles as well, but today she was dressed in a tight black sweater topping tight black jeans that were tucked into black leather boots.

She walked through the workroom to a small office in the back. She indicated that Ellie and I should take seats on the blue plastic chairs across the desk from where she sat down.

"I didn't kill Jason," she jumped right in.

"We know that," I answered. "The bartender at Lucky's already verified that you were at the bar during the time Jason was murdered."

Riley just looked at me as if to ask why in the heck I was bothering her if I already knew she wasn't the killer.

"The reason we're here is to find out if you have any information that might lead to the person who did kill the man," I continued.

"I thought you did."

"No," I corrected her. "I didn't kill Jason. At least I don't think I did. The whole thing was kind of a blur."

Riley laughed. Based on her stoic demeanor to that point, her reaction surprised me. "I sure hope you don't end up in jail. The DA is going to eat you alive."

"I don't plan to go to jail. I plan to find out who actually killed Jason. Is there anything you can tell me that might help me do that?"

Riley looked me up and down. I was sure she found me lacking, but I still hoped she'd point me in some direction.

"If I was investigating this case," she began, "I'd talk to five people." She took out a pen and paper and jotted down the names. She pushed the note across the desk. "If I were a betting woman, and I am, I'd bet you'll find your killer among the names on this list."

I picked up the paper and looked at it.

"Andrew Dover?" I asked.

"Andrew is the lead contractor working on the mall project. He hired Jason based on Billy Sand's recommendation. On the surface it appeared Jason was doing a passable job, but what neither Billy nor Andrew knew was that Jason was stealing materials from the project and selling them down in Bryton Lake."

"I suppose that could make this Andrew mad. Certainly mad enough to fire Jason, but kill him?"

"The thing is, Andrew isn't the one who noticed the discrepancy in materials. The investor developing the project did. Andrew almost lost his job over the whole thing. The only reason he didn't was because he promised to pay the guy back for the materials Jason took."

I could see how that might make a man mad enough to commit murder. It sounded like Jason got off scot-free. I asked Riley about that and she said she didn't know the details of the agreement the men came to.

"Kelly Arlington?" I asked as I considered the second name.

"I take it you already know Jason pretty much used her as a punching bag," Riley pointed out.

"Yeah, but I'm pretty sure she was passed out when Jason was stabbed." Actually, Salinger had pointed out that she could have come to and stabbed him after I passed out, but we didn't have any evidence to support that. "Why do you think she might have killed him after putting up with his abuse all that time?"

"She tried to kill him once before."

I frowned. "What do you mean?"

Riley leaned back in her chair. "Jason told me that Kelly ground up a lethal dose of sleeping pills and put them in his whiskey. The only reason he didn't die was because she had second thoughts after he drank the deadly brew and rushed him to the hospital to have his stomach pumped."

"So why wasn't she arrested?" Ellie asked.

"No one other than Jason knew what really happened. They told the cops and the doctor it was an accidental overdose. The only reason I know what really happened is because he told me after Kelly kicked him out a while back."

I took a minute to let this all sink in. Kelly had tried to kill Jason once. Could she have decided to try again? She certainly had more of a motive for wanting him dead than anyone else we had looked into.

I glanced down at the list. "Bram Willard? The same Bram Willard who owns the local feed store?"

"One and the same."

"But he's so nice. I really don't see him as the type to kill a man."

"Jason hooked up with Bram's sister Jennifer three nights before the fire. They met up at Lucky's and things progressed from there. I saw her in town on the morning of the fire and she had a huge bruise on her face. I don't know for a fact that Jason is responsible for that bruise, but based on what I know about the guy it seems likely."

Bram was a sweet man who I frequently chatted with when I stopped in to buy dog and cat food. He didn't seem like the violent type, but I had to admit he was protective of his sister, who had a bit of a wild side. I hoped he wasn't the killer, but the more I thought about it, the more I was convinced that he very well could be.

"Blugo? I don't know anyone named Blugo."

"You wouldn't. He tends to keep to himself."

"Do you know where we can find him or do you have a last name?"

"Tizzy will know where he hangs out."

Tisdale Brenton was the owner of Tizzy's Tats.

"So why do you think this Blugo might have killed Jason?" I asked.

"'Cause Jason won big at a poker game Blugo sat in on. Really big. A couple of days later Blugo found out that Jason had cheated. The idiot actually bragged about cheating to his bar mates after he'd had a few. I don't know Blugo all that well—no one really does—but I do know that cheating the man out of his money is as good as a death sentence."

"So you think he could have done it?" I mused.

"I think everyone on that list could have done it. That's why I gave you the names."

Riley made a good point.

"How do you know all this stuff?"

"I hang out in the bar. People talk; I listen."

I guess that made sense. I looked back down at the sheet of paper I held in my hands.

"Tina Littleton?" I read the last name out loud.

"The chick is a wacko," Riley began. "She had a thing with Jason prior to him and me hooking up, and when he tried to break it off she went psycho. She totally blamed me for the whole thing and started following me around."

Tina had admitted that she'd taken to stalking Riley after Jason broke things off with her. Still, it seemed if she was going to kill someone it would be Riley and not Jason she'd stab.

"I have to ask, if you knew the guy was an abuser and a cheater, why did you spend time with him?"

Riley shrugged. "I spend time with a lot of guys, and Jason could be a lot of fun. He only hit the weak and needy women in his life, so I never felt threatened. Besides, there was no way Jason was going to hit me and live to talk about it and he knew it, so he left me alone."

"Okay, well, thank you for the list." I stood up. "I do appreciate the information."

"Just don't tell anyone I gave it to you. It'd be bad for my badass reputation if anyone found out I was working with the sheriff."

"So what do you think?" Ellie asked after we left the shop and returned to the car, where the dogs were waiting.

"I'm not sure. I definitely want to talk to both Andrew and Bram, and it might not hurt to talk to Kelly again. Riley isn't the only one to suggest that Kelly could have woken up and killed Jason. Salinger said as much as well. I suppose we can stop by Tizzy's to see if he knows where to find this Blugo, and I still want to talk to Wiley about the fire. I stopped by the firehouse yesterday to ask him about fostering a few of our golden retriever pups, but he was off."

"Let's head back to the boathouse and drop off the dogs," Ellie said. "I promised Scooter's teacher I'd bring his costume in before lunch. We can do that and then get a bite to eat. After that we can go talk to Kelly together. I know her better than you do, so I might better be able to tell if she's lying. After we talk to her we can figure out our next move."

Chapter 6

Ellie and I decided to try out the new Mexican restaurant that had just opened a few weeks before. It was colorfully decorated in bright reds and greens, and the smell of spicy food cooking was enough to make my stomach rumble in anticipation of the enchiladas I planned to order.

"If the food tastes as good as it smells we're in for a real treat," Ellie commented.

"I agree, although I do miss your homemade soups."

"The next time I make soup I'll bring some over," Ellie promised. "I was thinking of making Zak's favorite casserole as a thank-you."

"Thank you?" I asked.

"Zak not only hired an attorney to deal with the insurance company for me but he put an indecent amount of money into my checking account so I wouldn't run short while we're getting everything worked out. I tried to tell him I couldn't take his money, but you know Zak; he insisted."

"Zak loves you. He wants to help. We both do. And we both feel bad about what happened to the restaurant."

"It's not your fault."

I shrugged. We'd danced this dance before and I saw little point in going over the same arguments again.

"Hopefully your claim will be settled in time for you to break ground on the new restaurant in the spring, as soon as the snow melts. It's going to be tough if you miss the summer building season."

"Actually, I'm not sure I'm going to rebuild," Ellie informed me.

"Not rebuild? Why?"

"When I first decided to open the restaurant I saw it as a way to get out from under my mom's shadow. But owning a restaurant is hard work and extremely time consuming. I guess I didn't really understand how many hours I'd have to put into the place. I realize I should have had a better understanding of the time commitment, given the fact that I was brought up in the restaurant business and my mom has always worked a lot of hours. But in the back of my mind, my little business was going to be a quarter of the size of Rosie's and would therefore, I figured, require a quarter of the time and effort to run it. Boy, was I wrong. If anything, I think I worked longer hours than Mom because she can afford more help than I could."

I frowned. "I've known you a long time and I've never known you to be afraid of hard work. I get that you might have had to work longer hours than you planned, but the Ellie I grew up with has always been willing to do what it takes to make her dreams come true."

"That's the thing—I'm not sure that owning my own business is my dream any longer. Now that I'm back to thinking about having a child, I'm realizing that I don't want a job that's so totally consuming. To be honest, I was kicking around the idea of selling even before this happened."

"I had no idea."

"I didn't say anything because I wasn't sure what I wanted to do. I talked to Zak for a bit and he assured me that at a minimum I'll get enough from the insurance to pay off the loan I took out to buy the place. I'll still have the land to sell, which should give me enough to start over with something new."

"Wow." Ellie and I were best friends and she'd never once mentioned that she was anything but thrilled with the Beach Hut. I had to wonder what else she hadn't been telling me. I guess we had drifted apart a bit once Zak came into my life.

"I still haven't decided for sure, and so far you and Zak are the only two who know what I'm thinking, so I'd appreciate it if you didn't say anything until I can make up my mind."

"Certainly. I won't say a word. Have you discussed this with Levi?"

"No. Not yet."

The fact that she'd told both Zak and me and not Levi really did seem to indicate that the romance between them might be in trouble.

The conversation paused as the waitress set our food in front of us. It looked as good as it smelled. The tortillas were handmade each day and the sauces were mixed on-site.

I'd just taken my first bite when I received a text from Jeremy, letting me know that someone had left a dog crate with a mama cat and six kittens on the stoop at the shelter. He wanted to know if Alex would be willing to foster the family until the kittens were old enough to adopt out. I texted back that I would ask her, but I was certain she'd be more than willing.

"Sorry," I apologized to Ellie because I was basically ignoring her. "I need to text Alex really quick. Kitten emergency."

"Everything okay?"

I explained about the cats left on our doorstep.

"Who would do a thing like that? It's freezing outside. What if Jeremy hadn't found them right away?"

"I agree that it seems like the responsible thing to do would have been to bring them inside, but there are some people who just don't want to take responsibility. At least they brought them to the shelter rather than just abandoning them somewhere."

Alex texted back, saying that she would be thrilled to foster, so I let Jeremy know that I'd pick the kittens up later in the day.

"So where were we?" I asked after I returned my attention to my food and my conversation with Ellie.

"I was about to ask you whether you wanted to head to Tizzy's first after we eat or go directly over to Kelly's?"

"Tizzy's is closer, and the feed store isn't all that much farther. We can head over to talk to Tizzy about this Blugo and then go to the feed store to talk to Bram. After that we can stop by Kelly's. I need to pick Scooter up from school, so that will probably be it for the day. Are you coming to Scooter's play tonight?"

"I'm not sure. I'm supposed to have dinner with Levi, if he doesn't end up canceling. I'm going to try to pin him down as to what's going on. It's hard to say how that conversation will go or how long it will take."

I placed my hand over Ellie's and gave it a squeeze. I wished I had the perfect thing to say but I didn't, so I just let her know by my actions that I was there for her should she need me.

Tizzy's Tats was a colorful place offering piercings as well as ink services. Tizzy was a small, well-groomed man in his midforties who didn't sport any visible piercings and only a couple of small tattoos, which was odd for a man in his profession. In spite of the fact that he didn't look the part of a tattoo artist, he had the reputation for being skilled in his profession.

"What can I do for you girls today? Maybe a lip ring for the holidays?"

"We aren't here for any body art today," I said. "We really just wanted to ask if you know a man named Blugo."

"Yeah, I know him."

"Does Blugo have a last name?" I wondered.

"Dunno. And I'm pretty sure Blugo isn't his real first name."

"Have you seen him lately?" I asked.

"No. He used to live in that rundown apartment building south of town, but I haven't seen him for weeks, so he might have left the area. I got the impression he was a man who liked to move around a lot."

"I guess you heard about Jason Overland," I continued.

"Yeah, I heard. Guy was a snake."

So far every person I'd talked to had referred to Jason as a snake or some other equally unpleasant equivalent. It was almost surprising that someone hadn't whacked him sooner.

"I heard Jason might have cheated Blugo out of some money. Does Blugo seem the type to seek revenge for something like that?"

"Hell yeah. Everyone knows you don't mess with Blugo. If Jason cheated Blugo he's as good as dead."

"He is dead," I reminded him.

"So he is. Maybe Blugo didn't leave town after all. It's hard to tell with him. The guy tends to keep to his own timetable. If I were you I wouldn't go looking for the guy. He won't take kindly to someone poking around in his business."

"I'll keep that in mind."

"So what now?" Ellie asked as we returned to the car.

"I'll call Salinger to give him the information we have regarding Blugo and then we can have our chat with Bram."

"Do you think Bram could actually kill someone for messing with his sister?"

"I don't know. I hope not. I like the guy, but I have noticed that he seems overly protective of Jennifer. I know she's gotten herself into some trouble in the past and I'm sure he's probably just trying to help her keep her life on track, but I've overheard a few conversations between the pair that sound more like a parent speaking to a child than one sibling speaking to another."

Willard's Feed had been a staple in Ashton Falls since before I was born. Bram's grandfather had opened the store at about the same time my own grandfather started Donovan's, the general store my dad now ran. Bram's father had taken over for his grandfather initially, but after suffering a fall on the ice five years ago, he'd decided to move to a warmer climate, leaving Bram in charge of both the store and his wild child sister.

As were all the other retail businesses in Ashton Falls, Willard's was decked out in red and green for the holiday. Perhaps I'd pick up some new toys for the Christmas stockings of all the Donovan-Zimmerman animals while I was there. I'd been meaning to stop by anyway and buying the gifts would give me a good excuse to start up a conversation.

"Those have been real popular this year." Bram walked up behind me while I sorted through the catnip toys shaped like candy canes, snowmen, and wreaths.

"They're pretty cute. I think all of our cats will have to have at least one."

"I have something similar for dogs two aisles over."

"Thanks; I'll head there next." I smiled at him.

"I noticed Ellie came in with you. I wanted to let her know that the brand of dog food she feeds Shep is on special this month. Figured she might want to stock up while the sale is on."

"I'll tell her. I think she went to look at dog beds in the back."

"Shame about her restaurant," Bram offered. "It was one of my favorite places to grab a bite."

"It did seem to be a local favorite. I guess you heard Jason Overland died in that fire."

"I heard." Bram's lips tightened. "I was sorry to hear about the building but not a bit sorry to hear about the fact that someone saved me the trouble of killing the guy."

"I know what happened to Jennifer," I said gently. "Was she hurt bad?"

"Bad enough. What she ever saw in the guy I will never know. I warned her to stay away from the loser, but she isn't one to listen to her big brother. When I saw what that monster had done to her face I wanted to kill him. Would have, too, but like I said, someone beat me to it. If you figure out who it was thank him for me."

"Kelly Arlington and I almost died in that fire as well," I reminded the man who, it seemed, wasn't quite the nice guy I'd thought he was.

"Yeah, I heard about that. If it had been me who killed the thug who hit Jennifer, I wouldn't have left the two of you there to die. I suppose the person who killed Jason was a bigger monster than he was, to be willing to sacrifice innocent lives the way he did."

Bram had a point. We were looking for a killer who not only had a grudge against

Jason but the moral deficiency to allow two innocent people die. Somehow I didn't think anyone on my list fit that description.

"Just in case you're wondering, I was here at the store when the whole thing went down," Bram offered. "There are two clerks who can vouch for the fact that I didn't leave all day. Saturday's are my busiest days."

Ellie and I headed over to talk to Kelly. It turned out to be a short but emotional conversation. Kelly admitted to putting sleeping pills in Jason's whiskey in a moment of weakness, but then assured us that she had regretted it immediately and would never have attempted something like that again. I wasn't 100 percent sure I believed her, but she did seem sincere in her assurance that she hadn't killed Jason.

After we left Kelly we headed over to speak with Tina Littleton, who again admitted to stalking Riley when Jason first broke up with her but swore that her love for Jason was in the past and she hadn't given him a thought in months.

"What now?" Ellie asked after we finished with Tina.

"I need to pick Scooter up in half an hour and I wanted to drive around the neighborhood where Cupcake went missing to tack up some flyers on stop signs and telephone poles, so I guess I'll take you home."

"Cupcake?"

I explained about the missing dog and the little girl who had asked Santa for a Christmas miracle.

"Wow, I hope you find the dog. How awful to lose a beloved pet so soon after losing your mother."

"I really want to find this dog, but I have to admit the odds aren't good. She's been missing for a long time. Besides, it's been snowing off and on for over a week. Unless she found someone to take her in I'm afraid a little dog like Cupcake might have succumbed to the cold."

"I'll keep an eye out for her," Ellie promised. "In fact, I'll take some of those flyers and pass them out during Hometown Christmas this weekend. Someone has to have seen her."

Later that evening, Zak and I sat nervously in the community center waiting for Scooter's play to begin. Pi was hanging out with friends and Alex was sitting with Phyllis and the girls with whom she shared her home. I'd told Zak the outcome of my afternoon's sleuthing while we worked together to clean the kitchen after dinner. Ellie and I had given it our best shot, but it turned out we weren't any closer to solving the case than we'd been that morning.

"I can't believe how nervous I am," I said to Zak. "I realize Scooter is only an elf and he doesn't even have any lines, but I still feel butterflies in my stomach."

"Me too. I can't help but have flashbacks to my own Christmas play when I was in the fourth grade."

"Were you an elf too?"

"The Christmas tree. And, like Scooter. I didn't have any lines. All I had to do was walk out onto the stage and stand there, but the costume only had a small opening for me to look out and I couldn't see very well. I tripped over someone's foot and fell flat on my face."

"Oh, no." I laughed. "Were you embarrassed?"

"Traumatized was more like it. Like this play, mine was held on the Friday evening before winter break and I spent the next two weeks trying to convince my mom that we should move to another school district."

"I take it you were unsuccessful."

"I was. But as it turned out, all my angst was for nothing. By the time we returned to school everyone had forgotten about the play and the subject of my pratfall never came up."

The lights dimmed.

I took Zak's hand in mine and gave it a squeeze. I really hoped Scooter didn't trip. Maybe he would recover, but I wasn't sure I ever would. I'd never really understood why my dad would get so nervous when I had athletic or academic competitions as a child until I became a surrogate mother. The desire for your child to be successful really is an all-encompassing yearning that I would be willing to bet is built into our adult DNA.

Chapter 7

Saturday, December 19

Today hadn't gone at all as planned. I'd meant to spend the day with the family at Hometown Christmas, enjoying the festivities with a little sleuthing on the side; instead, a huge storm blew in, knocking out power to the entire area and effectively closing down the town. The community center was powered by backup generators, so everyone gathered together whatever food and drink they felt they could donate and headed to the large building for an impromptu community feast.

Zak, Levi, and a few other men were out in their four-wheel-drive trucks rescuing people who had gotten stuck in the snow and checking on elderly and disabled community members.

Tawny Upton, along with a few other moms, were entertaining the younger children, and Ellie and a few other culinarily gifted individuals took charge of combining the ingredients that had been donated into delicious-looking soups, casseroles, and side dishes.

I, not possessing any special talent, was helping out and filling in where I could.

"Zoe, why don't you go ahead and start taking out the salads we have ready?" Ellie instructed. "I think we'll serve in courses. Soups and salads first, followed by casseroles and sides, and finally the desserts."

"Are the soups going to be ready in time?" I asked.

"Yeah, they'll be ready. We made stovetop soups that didn't require a lot of cooking time. We can heat the casseroles in the ovens while everyone is enjoying the soup and salad portion of the meal, so we should be able to segue smoothly between courses."

"And the bread?" Phyllis King asked.

"Let's heat it and serve it with the soups and salads," Ellie decided. "Hazel, why don't you check the refrigerator for any chilled salads? I know several people brought some they'd already prepared. And why don't a couple of you find large bowls to serve the green salads in? I think there are extra serving pieces in the basement."

"I'll go," I offered. It was getting hot and crowded in the kitchen, and as much as I was enjoying this time with some of my favorite people, the idea of a few minutes to myself seemed wonderful about now.

"I'll go with you," Jeremy said. He had been making spaghetti sauce, which was now simmering on the stove.

"It's really coming down," I said as I looked out the window Jeremy and I passed on our way to the stairs. All that was visible was a sheet of white. The snow had been coming down like that for most of the day. The town had plows out trying to keep up with the snowfall, but I imagined, unless the storm let up, we were going to be spending the night with the friends and neighbors with whom we had gathered to share a meal.

Of course I had a huge truck that I'd had the foresight to drive into town, so chances were the Donovan-Zimmerman clan would be able to make it home. I'd gone back to the house earlier to check on the animals and had had little trouble navigating the deep drifts of snow that covered the roads.

"Yeah, it really is," Jeremy agreed. "I feel like I should head over to the Zoo to check on things. The generators had kicked in when I left to pick up Morgan, Phyllis, and the girls, but Tank hadn't shown up yet and he's still not answering his cell."

Tank River was one of two brothers who worked the graveyard shift at Zoe's Zoo.

"I'll go with you after we get the dishes Ellie wants. I could use some fresh air."

"Have you heard from Zak and the rescue crew?" Jeremy asked as we started down the stairs.

"Not for a couple of hours. The last I heard they were trying to talk Mrs. Broomsfield into coming into town with them."

Mrs. Broomsfield was an elderly woman who lived alone with only her cat, Madeline, for company.

"I imagine she didn't want to leave Madeline alone."

"Exactly. And I can't say that I really blame her. I'm not thrilled about leaving my menagerie alone, but I've snuck back home a few times to check on them and they're fine."

Jeremy clicked on the overhead light when we'd made it to the bottom of the stairs. "Does Mrs. Broomsfield have a generator?"

"No, and her heat is electric, which was why Zak wanted her to come into town. He's worried about leaving her alone without a source of heat."

Jeremy picked up several large bowls and began to sort them into a pile. "Maybe you can talk her into taking Madeline over to your place to hang out with your animals and then coming into town for some food."

"That's a good idea. We can close Madeline into one of the bedrooms if we need to. I'm not sure how well she'll like all our dogs. Not only are my three at the house but Ellie brought Shep over and Levi dropped Karloff off on his way into town as well. I'll text Zak to suggest it, although he hasn't answered the last two texts I've sent him," I continued. "I imagine cell reception could be sketchy in some of the more isolated areas."

I grabbed as many bowls as I could carry and Jeremy picked up his stack and we headed back up the stairs.

"Maybe we can stop by to pick her up after we check on the animals at the Zoo," Jeremy suggested.

"Good idea. I won't even bother Zak with it. I'm sure he has his hands full rescuing stranded motorists."

We told Ellie what we were doing and promised Phyllis we would stop off to check on the two cats who lived in her house, then Jeremy and I set off into the storm. Living in the mountains, I was used to winter storms, and even somewhat used to blizzards, but the snow had to be falling at the rate of several inches an hour. The main roads were passable, but it was going to be hard to navigate the side roads even with my big truck.

We arrived at the Zoo to find the generators pumping and Tank and his brother Gunnar warm and toasty, sharing a night cap and playing a game of cards. They assured us they'd checked the fuel for the generators and had plenty, and both planned to sleep on the cots we provided for just that purpose.

When we were satisfied that things were under control at the Zoo, Jeremy and I went by to check on the cats at Phyllis's and then headed toward Mrs. Broomsfield's house. It was slow going with all the snow, so we passed the time catching each other up on the events of the past few days. I began by filling him in on the investigation into Jason Overland's death and the progress, or perhaps I should say lack of progress, that I'd made.

"Who have you definitely eliminated by confirming an alibi?" Jeremy asked as I struggled to find the road markers.

"Bram Willard said he was working. I didn't actually speak to the clerks he assured me would vouch for him, but it doesn't make sense he would provide me with an alibi if he was lying. I'm pretty sure I can cross him off the list, though he was pretty open about his desire to do away with the man. I suppose he could have hired someone to do it."

"True, but by that logic anyone could have hired someone. For now, let's just assume that a firm alibi will eliminate a suspect. Watch out for that tree."

I swerved to avoid a tree that was down in the middle of the road. Luckily, I was going slowly because I hadn't seen it until I was almost upon it.

"The bartender at Lucky's confirmed that Riley was there until midnight, so we can eliminate her," I continued. "I didn't think to ask Tina about an alibi, but I'll work it into the conversation when I see her next. Kelly was passed out on the floor when I blacked out, but Salinger pointed out that she could have woken up and stabbed Jason, then passed out again. Still, someone set the fire and I really doubt it was her, so I'm inclined to believe she didn't do it. Besides, she was pretty beaten up; it's unlikely she would have been able to overpower Jason to stab him."

"I don't know. Rage has a way of making you stronger than you normally would be," Jeremy pointed out. "I wouldn't totally discount the idea that Kelly could have regained consciousness, stabbed Jason, and then passed out again, but you're correct in thinking she most likely wouldn't have started the fire."

"I guess I can move Kelly to the maybe list. She seems an unlikely suspect, but the more we discuss this the more I can see that it isn't impossible that she could have killed Jason."

"Okay, so you have Tina on the list without a confirmed alibi. Who else?" Jeremy asked as I slowly turned onto the street where Mrs. Broomsfield lived.

"I haven't had the opportunity to speak to Andrew Dover. His was one of the names Riley gave me."

"I know Andrew. He's at the community center. I saw him there earlier. It's doubtful he'll leave before we get back. You can talk to him then. Anyone else?"

I told Jeremy about Blugo, who seemed exactly the type to kill someone, though no one had seen him around as of late. I'd driven by the apartment Tizzy had given me, but it had been dark every time.

"Did you see that?" I asked Jeremy as we pulled up in front of Mrs. Broomsfield's house.

"See what?"

"Something black just ran under the truck parked in the driveway across the street. I only saw it because it ran under a house light. It must be battery operated. You go in and check on Mrs. Broomsfield; I'm going to check over there."

"Probably just a cat," Jeremy said. "I'm sure it'll be fine under the car."

"I still haven't found Cupcake. I have to be sure."

Jeremy got out of the truck and slowly made his way up the unshoveled walk while I headed across the street. I knelt down and tried to peer under the body of the vehicle, but it was too dark.

"Cupcake?" I called.

An animal whimpered.

"Come on out, sweetie. If you do I'll take you home."

It took a few minutes, but by the time Jeremy returned to the truck with Mrs. Broomsfield and her cat, I had a scrawny black dog, who I hoped was Cupcake, in my arms.

"I see you managed to catch the pie thief," Mrs. Broomsfield commented as I passed the dog to Jeremy, who had slid into the backseat so the elderly woman could sit in the front.

"Pie thief?"

"Little scamp stole the pie I had cooling on the outdoor table a couple of weeks ago."

"I think he's the dog a little girl who lives a few blocks over is looking for. Do you mind if we stop by to check with her before we head over to my house with Madeline?"

"Fine by me."

Luckily, I had driven this neighborhood many times over the past week and knew exactly where Tabitha lived. I crossed my fingers and headed up to the front porch. The house was dark, but I could see smoke coming out of the chimney, and it looked as if there were candles burning in a room at the front.

I knocked and waited.

"Can I help you?" a man, who I assumed was Tabitha's father, answered.

"My name is Zoe Donovan. I own the animal shelter in town. I know your daughter has been looking for her dog. Is this her?"

The man gave me a funny look. "You own the animal shelter?"

"I do."

"And you can't tell the difference between a girl dog and a boy dog?"

I turned the dog over. Talk about being embarrassed. I'd been so excited to find the dog I was sure was Cupcake that I hadn't even checked.

"I guess not," I admitted. "I'm sorry to have bothered you."

Jeremy laughed for a good ten minutes when I returned to the truck and told him what had happened. I threatened him with all sorts of horrible consequences if he told anyone about my blunder. He said he wouldn't, but knowing him, he probably would.

By the time Jeremy recovered from laughing we'd arrived at my house. I'd planned to simply drop Madeline off and then continue on to the community center, but Mrs. Broomsfield insisted on staying at the house with the animals. Thanks to the generator, the house was warm and toasty and we had plenty of food on hand, so I didn't really have an argument. Zak must have come by with the plow crew because even our drive had been cleared. I fed the dog I'd found and introduced him to the pack of dogs at the house. They seemed to get along fine, so I gave Mrs. Broomsfield instructions on how to use Zak's fancy video player and what to do should the generator go out, and then headed back to the community center with Jeremy.

"I can't believe that dog wasn't Cupcake," I mused as we made our way out onto the recently plowed highway. "Same size, same color, same part of town."

"Hopefully the dog didn't live at the house you took it from," Jeremy said.

"Yeah, me too. He was pretty thin. I'm betting he's a stray, but we can work it all out once the storm passes. I hope we can find a place to park that isn't under two feet of snow."

"Let's just park in the no parking zone in the front. I'm betting it's been cleared, and if there's an emergency your truck is probably the best equipped to handle the road conditions."

We parked and I headed to the kitchen to check in with Ellie. Almost everyone in attendance was sitting at the long tables that had been set up, catching up on local events and enjoying the food that had been served. From the festive atmosphere in the room, you'd never guess there was a blizzard raging outside that had totally closed down all roads into and out of Ashton Falls.

The long-range forecast called for clearing after midnight. I just hoped the crews could get the roads clear enough for everyone to get home safely. Of course there was still the situation with the electricity. Those without either gas or wood-burning stoves were going to be in trouble if the power company didn't get it back on.

"It looks like your first course was a hit," I said to Ellie and the other women in the kitchen.

"Yeah, it doesn't look like we'll have leftovers," Ellie commented. "I'm going to need someone to clear the empty serving bowls from the table and give them a quick scrub so we can make room for the casseroles and sides."

"I'm on it," I volunteered. "Have you seen or heard from Zak and the others?"

"A couple of the guys came in to warm up and grab some food, but I haven't seen either Zak or Levi."

"Knowing Zak, he won't stop to take a break until everyone is safe and sound. I just hope the snow stops soon and the electricity is restored so everyone can go home this evening."

"The plow guys who came in said the power company is working on the problem and hopes to have power restored by midnight. Still, that's a long time to keep everyone entertained."

"I'll talk to Gilda about organizing some of the older kids to do a performance of some sort," I offered.

Gilda Reynolds was the owner of a local gift shop and the leader of the community theater. If anyone could figure out a way to keep the masses entertained, it was Gilda.

"That's a good idea."

"There are some cards and board games in the basement. I saw them when I went to fetch the serving bowls. Maybe we can pass them out after we finish eating."

I spent the next twenty minutes bringing empty dishes in from the first course and replacing them with delicious-looking casseroles and side dishes. I hadn't had a chance to eat myself and fully intended to do so, but first I was going to take the opportunity I'd been provided to speak to Andrew Dover when he went out into the storm for a smoke.

Chapter 8

"It's quite some storm," I said conversationally when I'd bundled up and joined Andrew Dover under the covered entry.

"Biggest snow I can remember and I've lived here almost ten years."

Andrew took a long drag on his cigarette, followed by a long exhale that filled the area with smoke. I tried not to cough but was unsuccessful.

"Smoke bothering you?" Andrew asked.

"No. It's fine. I was in a fire a week ago and I'm still a little sensitive to smoke, I guess." I took a step back.

"Heard about that fire." Andrew took another drag on his cigarette but turned his head to blow the smoke away from where I was standing.

"I guess you know that Jason Overland died in the fire."

"I heard."

"I remember his girlfriend, Kelly, mentioning that he used to work for you."

Andrew laughed. "Is that why you're hanging out here in the blizzard, choking on cigarette smoke rather than being inside where it's warm? You wanted to ask me about Jason?"

"Yeah," I admitted. "I guess I did."

"You think I killed him?"

"Did you?"

"Sherriff Salinger asked me that same question. I'll tell you the same thing I told him: The guy was a complete and total moron. I gave him a job when no one else would and he repaid me by stealing from the site. I almost lost my job over that, and I'll be paying my boss back for what Jason stole for the next year. I hated the guy, but no, I didn't kill him. I was up on the mountain skiing when the guy was whacked. I was with four other guys; you can check. I already gave Salinger the list of names."

"I'm sorry. I should have checked with Salinger before I bothered you. He didn't mention that he'd spoken to you the last time I checked in with him."

Andrew took one last drag on his cigarette, then tossed it on the ground before grinding it out with his boot. "Look, I get that you want to find out what happened. To be honest, I'm curious as well. There are three or four guys who come to mind as possibly having a motive. I gave Salinger the names. I know he's out dealing with the snow situation, but maybe once this storm clears the two of you can sit down and have yourselves a nice chat. As for me, I'm heading in to get my share of the main course before it's gone."

With that, Andrew went inside.

I remained on the deck for a few more minutes, trying to clear my head. It was cold outside, but I had on knee-high winter boots, heavy jeans, a thick sweater, and a down jacket. I was quickly running out of suspects. If neither Dover nor Bram did it that just left Kelly, Tina, and Blugo on Riley's list. Riley had seemed so confident that one of the five people was guilty of the murder. Of the three who were left, Blugo seemed the most likely, but so far I hadn't been able to track him down. For all I knew he'd left town before the murder even occurred.

Riley had said that Blugo was angry at Jason because he'd cheated him out of money at a poker game. If that was true, there had to have been other people playing in the same game who had also been cheated. Maybe one of them knew where I could find Blugo or, better yet, maybe one of them was as mad as Blugo about getting cheated and had taken his own revenge. I had no idea how I was going to find out who those people were, but I had half the town sequestered in one place. It certainly couldn't hurt to ask around.

Before returning inside I took out my phone. Still no response from Zak. It wasn't like him not to return my texts, so I had to assume he was still out of range. I tried to call his cell, but it just went to voice mail. I decided to leave a message.

"Hey, it's me. Just checking in. There's a bunch of really awesome-looking food over here at the community center. You and Levi should stop by for a bite. Give me a call when you get this message. If you're out of range to call, try a text. Love you."

I knew I shouldn't be worried about Zak. He was the most capable person I had ever met. But both the rescue crew and the road crew had been filtering in to warm up and eat, and the fact that neither Zak nor Levi had shown up was beginning to concern me nonetheless.

As I walked back through the crowd, I couldn't help but smile. In spite of the less than desirable reason for the gathering everyone seemed to be having a wonderful time. The room had been decked out in red and green and there was a twenty-foot tree standing in one corner, giving the room a festive air. Holiday tunes played in the background as neighbors caught up on the latest news.

"Good turnout," the bartender from Lucky's commented when I walked over to the buffet table.

"It is. It seems all you need to ensure a full house is a town-wide power outage. I take it the electricity is out at the bar as well."

"Yup. Did you ever find out who whacked Jason?"

"Not yet. I did find out that he cheated someone named Blugo out of some money in a poker game."

The bartender raised his eyebrows. "Takes guts to do that. Sounds to me like you have your killer. If Jason cheated Blugo, he was as good as dead."

"Several other people have said the same thing. The problem is that I haven't been able to track the guy down."

"Trust me, little thing like you doesn't want to try. The guy will eat you alive. Best you let sleeping dogs lie in this instance."

"Perhaps." I nodded. "But it occurred to me that if Jason was cheating at poker Blugo wasn't the only one to fall victim. There had to have been other players."

The bartender plopped an olive in his mouth and chewed slowly. "True. Still, if I were you I'd leave it alone."

"You're probably right, but if I did want to speak to the other men who were playing, any idea who I should talk to?"

The bartender stared at me. "You really aren't going to leave this alone, are you?"

I shrugged.

"It's your funeral. If you want to find out who participated in the game talk to Scully."

"Scully?"

The bartender nodded toward an older man who was slight in stature and didn't appear to have a violent bone in his body.

"The guy talking to that tall blond lady over near the Christmas tree?"

"Yup. Scully runs most of the illegal gambling in the area. If Jason was involved in a high-stakes game Scully would know about it."

"Okay, thanks. You've been very helpful."

"If by helpful you mean I just signed your death warrant by putting you on to the man who might know where Blugo is then, yeah, I've been real helpful."

I had to admit at that point there was a little voice in my head telling me to leave things alone. I thought of Zak and how scared he'd been when I'd almost died—again. I remembered my promise to him, and in that moment I really wanted to be the wife he deserved. I took out my phone, called Salinger's number, gave him Scully's name, and then headed to the kitchen to do what I was actually there to do: help neighbors in need.

"Oh, good, you're back," Ellie greeted me as soon as I walked into the kitchen. "A group of emergency personnel are taking a break in the firehouse and I told them I'd send some food over there. I have it packaged up if you wouldn't mind delivering it."

"I'd be happy to."

"The firehouse is just down the street, but I think you should take someone with you. I'm sure it's possible to get stuck even with your monster truck."

"I'll grab Jeremy."

"Why don't you grab something to eat and I'll find him?" Ellie offered. "You've been running around all day and I'm willing to bet you haven't eaten a thing."

Ellie wasn't wrong, so I made myself a quick plate while she tracked down Jeremy and had the food she'd prepared loaded onto my truck. Combining a bite of this with a bite of that was delicious.

Alex approached from across the room. I hadn't kept track of any of the kids since we'd been at the community center, but there were plenty of adults around and we were in a building full of friends.

"Did you check on the kittens when you went out earlier?" Alex asked.

"I did and they're fine. Have you seen Scooter?"

"He's hanging out with Tucker and some of the other kids in his class. I think they're all going to help Mrs. Reynolds with some kind of performance."

"And Pi?"

"The last time I saw him he was with Brooklyn and some of the other kids from the high school. I think they're all in the little conference room in the back. I've been hanging out with Eve and Pepper, but when I saw you standing here I thought I'd ask about the kittens."

I put my arm around Alex. "You're such a good mom. Mrs. Broomsfield decided to stay at the house with the animals. She said she'd look in on them from time to time."

Alex let out a long breath. "Good. That makes me feel better. They're so little."

"Jeremy and I are heading back out to take some food over to the firehouse. If you see Scooter and Pi tell them I'll be back in a bit."

"Okay, I will." Alex trotted away.

I looked around the room for Jeremy. I wondered whether Zak and Levi might be at the firehouse. Ellie hadn't said, but if the emergency crew was taking a break, maybe the volunteers were as well. Jeremy waved to me from across the room to indicate that he was all loaded and ready to go. I waved back and headed in his direction.

"It looks like the snow is tapering off," he said as we drove slowly through the deserted town. "At least the visibility is a lot better than it was even a half hour ago."

"Yeah, it's quite a bit better. Maybe the plow guys can get caught up and folks can start heading home."

"We still have no power," Jeremy reminded me.

Jeremy had a point. Those with a wood fireplace or gas heat source would be fine, but Ashton Falls residents who depended on electricity to heat their homes would be better off staying at the community center for the duration.

It was an odd experience to drive through the middle of town when it was totally dark and completely deserted. I almost felt like I was in some post-apocalyptic sci-fi movie. The drive between the community center and the firehouse was a short one. I supposed someone must have let the guys know that food was on its way because there was a parking space all plowed out for us near the side door leading into the kitchen.

The guys had done a nice job decorating the firehouse. There were red and green lights around the windows that actually shone because the firehouse ran on backup generators. There was a tall tree in one corner of the main room that was decorated with a variety of things, including old cans and pieces of silverware.

After Jeremy and I helped the men unload my truck, I looked around for Wiley Holt. He was in the kitchen, filling large pitchers with ice water while the rest of the group were serving up plates of food from the buffet we'd set up.

"Hey, Wiley," I greeted him.

"Thanks for bringing the food. I think it's going to be a long night."

"Yeah, it looks like it. I know you're busy and want to get some of the food I brought before it's gone, but I wanted to ask you about the fire at Ellie's."

"Take a couple of those pitchers for me and we'll drop them off. I'll grab a plate of food and we can talk while I eat."

"Thanks. That sounds good."

I helped Wiley serve the water and then refilled serving dishes while he made up a plate. We found a place off to the side, where we could speak uninterrupted.

"So what's on your mind?" Wiley asked as he dug into the food.

"I know you were with the first responders and I guess I was just looking for a little clarification as to how and when the fire started."

He shoveled a few more bites of food into his mouth before he answered. I couldn't blame him; he'd probably been out in the storm for hours, helping stranded motorists and shut-ins isolated by the storm.

Wiley swallowed and took a sip of water before he began. "It appeared as if the fire started on the grill and spread from there. It could have been intentionally set or it could have been an accident."

"An accident?"

"It's feasible that the grill was left on and a flammable object such as a piece of paper or a napkin came into contact with the greasy surface and became enflamed. The real problem is that the fire burned through the wall behind the grill and entered the storage area, where a large quantity of fire starter was stored."

"Ellie uses the fire starter for the outdoor BBQs in the summer and the warming pits in the winter."

"Once the fire hit the accelerant the place went up quick. It was an old building and the wood walls and floors were nothing more than kindling for the fire. It's a good thing you got out when you did."

I took a minute to wrap my head around what Wiley was telling me while he shoveled more of his food into his mouth. "So it's possible that someone could have stabbed Jason and left and the fire could have started at some point after that?"

"Sure, it's possible. Hard to tell at this point if the killer set the fire to cover up any evidence that was left behind or if he somehow knocked something onto the hot grill but left before whatever it was burst into flame."

The possibility that the fire was an accident created a whole new list of suspects in my mind. Kelly Arlington, for one. It had been speculated that she'd come to and stabbed Jason, but I hadn't seen her setting fire to the place. What if she came to after Jason knocked me out, grabbed a knife—which could very well have been sitting on the counter, although I didn't specifically remember one being there—stabbed Jason, and then passed out once again? The fire started, I woke up, saw the flames, grabbed Kelly, and got us both out of there. I tried to remember the placement of Kelly's body during the course of the event. When I'd regained consciousness and seen the flames she was near the counter, not all that far from where Jason's body was. I tried to remember where she had initially fallen. The whole thing was still a blur, but it seemed to me that she was closer to the door than to the counter. As hard as I tried, I couldn't remember with any certainty, but the fact that the fire could have been an accident gave me a new train of thought to consider.

"Did you notice anything else that might help to explain what happened?" I asked.

"The place was already totally engulfed when we arrived. You were lying in the snow, not all that far from the building, next to Kelly. You were both unconscious. We had you transported to the hospital and then we worked to make certain the fire wouldn't spread to any nearby trees."

"So you didn't try to retrieve Jason's body at that point?"

"No. It was obvious that if anyone was inside the building they were already dead and it was much too dangerous to enter the building. This casserole is really good." Wiley shoveled another forkful of food into his mouth. "Tell Ellie thanks from all of us."

"I will. And thanks for the information. Did Jeremy call you about the puppies?"

"He did, and I have two of them at my house. Don't worry; my power runs on a generator so they're nice and toasty warm. I'm going to stop off to check on them when we head back out."

"Did you happen to see Zak and Levi when you were out and about today?" I asked. "They're in Zak's truck."

"I didn't see them, but I overheard one of the guy's mention that they were going to check on some of the folks who live off the old county road. It's pretty isolated out there with the electricity being off and all."

"Do you remember when that was?"

"Guessing about two hours ago or thereabouts."

"Even with the road conditions, that seems like a long time."

"I wouldn't worry. Zak and Levi both know how to deal with the snow and road conditions. Chances are they might have been invited in to one of the homes they went to check on to warm up. Most of the homes out there have wood stoves."

"Yeah, you're right. I shouldn't worry. Enjoy the rest of your dinner. Jeremy and I really should be getting back to the community center. I'm sure Ellie and the kitchen crew need our help."

After saying our good-byes, we headed back out to my truck.

"Wiley said Zak and Levi went to check on the residents who live off the old county road two hours ago. They really should be back by now. I'm getting worried that they might have slid off the road and are sitting in a ditch. I'm going to go look for them. I can drop you back at the community center if you'd prefer."

"If you're going out into the county in this storm I'm going with you. Let's let someone know where we're going, though, just in case *we* get stuck."

I called Ellie, who asked if she could come along after I informed her of our plans. The food had all been served and the natives were getting restless. She confessed that she was ready for some fresh air and a break from the noise and busyness of the community center. I told her to let Phyllis and a few others know where we were going and then meet us out in the front of the building. If everything was fine and Zak and Levi didn't need rescuing, we should be back in thirty minutes tops.

"Do you have a shovel and tow chain in the truck?" Jeremy asked.

I nodded. "I also have tire chains, and my dad gave the winch a tune-up before he left on his trip. There's no way we're getting stuck."

My dad had specially outfitted the truck I use when I first began working in animal rescue. It was not only large and heavy with a high clearance but he'd had it specially weighted to provide maximum traction. It was a four-wheel-drive monster that was close to impossible to find a parking space for but could handle pretty much any weather conditions you threw at it.

I pulled up in front of the community center, where Ellie was waiting. She climbed inside and I pulled back onto Main.

"Thanks for picking me up. I really needed a break from the ruckus."

"No problem," I answered. "It's pretty loud with so many people packed into such a small space."

"Yeah, it's really great that everyone has come together and seems to be having a great time, but with everyone talking at once it's louder in that building than a rock concert."

"Why do you think I keep volunteering for things that take me outside?"

I filled Jeremy and Ellie in on my conversation with Wiley as I slowly navigated the road out of town.

"Wow," Ellie responded. "The fire was an accident?"

"Maybe. Wiley wasn't certain, but based on the sequence of events it very well could have been."

"I'm honestly not sure if that makes me feel better or worse. If it was an accident, then my decision to keep the fire starter in the storeroom could be the primary reason the building was a total loss."

"Someone still had to have knocked something onto the grill and Kelly still had to have left the grill on," I pointed out.

"It is odd that Kelly would have left the grill on," Ellie commented. "She's usually pretty careful about that."

"What if she turned the grill on because she was going to make herself something to eat and then Jason came in and distracted her?" Jeremy suggested.

"I suppose it could have happened that way," Ellie said. "If the grill hadn't been cleaned yet there would be residual grease on it, and if a flammable object came into contact with it when it was hot it could have burst into flames."

"So if the fire was an accident are you back to thinking Kelly might have stabbed Jason?" Jeremy asked.

"I don't know. Maybe. She said she didn't, but she's also said on more than one occasion that she can't remember what happened from the time I first arrived until she woke up in the hospital. What if she woke up and saw me on the floor? Maybe she was just trying to protect me, or maybe Jason came after her and she was trying to protect herself. If there was a knife on the counter she would be the one to have put it there. Maybe she remembered the knife, grabbed it, stabbed Jason, and then passed out."

"What about the man you thought you saw?" Jeremy asked.

"I don't know. I feel like I remember someone else coming in, but it isn't clear, so I can't be certain. I wish the fog that's been hindering my memories would clear a bit."

I pulled off the main highway onto the old county road. The main highway leading out of town had been recently plowed and the snow had slowed considerably, so navigating wasn't too bad. The old road, which was only used by the local residents once the new one was built almost ten years ago, was an entirely different story. Luckily, there were snow poles to sort of identify the road; otherwise I would have ended up in someone's pasture more likely than not.

"I hope we don't get stuck," Ellie worried.

"If we do I'll winch us out."

I drove slowly as I tried to figure out exactly where the road ended and the shoulder began. The homes on this stretch of road were scattered pretty sparsely. It was as much as a quarter of a mile between driveways at some points. Most of the homes were dark, leading me to believe that the majority of the residents had gone into town before the snow got too deep. It took longer than I'd anticipated to make it to the end of the road. I was disappointed that we hadn't found Zak's truck. On the other hand, I was relieved that he hadn't gotten stuck. I pulled into the last driveway at the end of the road only to find Zak's truck parked in front of a mostly dark house. There was a slight flicker of light from the back of the house, which I assumed came from a wood fire and candles.

"I wonder what the guys are doing here," Ellie murmured.

"Isn't this where Hilary Fineland lives?" I asked.

"Yeah, I think it is," Jeremy answered.

Hilary was pregnant with her first child. She wasn't due for another month, so I really hoped everything was okay, but I did notice that her husband's truck wasn't in front of the house. Ellie, Jeremy, and I got out and approached the house.

The situation was exactly as I'd feared. Hilary was in labor and her husband, Jerry, who had gone for help because the phone wasn't working, had never come back.

"What can we do?" I asked Zak, who seemed to have taken charge of the situation.

"It looks like we're going to need to deliver this baby," Zak informed me. "It's much too late to leave here and I haven't been able to get through to Jerry to see if help is on the way."

I went into the room where Hilary was in bed. Tears were streaming down her face, although I wasn't certain whether they were the result of pain or fear or both.

I took the woman's hand in mine. "Hey, Hilary. Zak and I are going to help you deliver your baby and Ellie is going to help you with your breathing. I just need you to relax as much as you can."

"Do you know how to deliver a baby?"

"Actually, I delivered my sister Harper. It's easier than you think. I'm going to go wash my hands and Zak is going to gather a few supplies. Ellie is going to stay here with you, but we'll be back in just a few minutes."

"Okay." Hilary actually looked a bit more confident.

"Are you okay to do this?" Zak asked when we left the bedroom.

"Do we have a choice?"

"No," Zak admitted. "I guess not. How did you find us?"

"I got worried when I couldn't get hold of you so I came looking. Why didn't you just put her in your truck and take her into town?"

"The labor came on quick. Jerry was already gone when Levi and I stopped by. I was afraid she would deliver during the drive into town. I was also afraid we could get stuck. We talked about it and decided it was best just to stay put and hope for the best."

"Okay." I took a deep breath. "Let's do this."

Luckily, the labor was quick and the delivery problem-free. I stood back and watched Hilary as she cuddled her new baby. I could hear the sound of plows in the distance. Chances were help was finally on the way.

I couldn't help but notice Ellie watching Hilary. She had a smile on her face that didn't quite conceal a look of longing. I noticed Levi watching Ellie, and I couldn't help but see the look of sadness that washed over his face.

Chapter 9

Monday, December 21

If any of you have ever wondered what happens when you combine a hundred rolls of wrapping paper, twenty bags of bows, yards of ribbon, and twenty-seven eager helpers, the answer is total insanity. Granted it was the wonderful sort of insanity that occurred when people you loved came together to lend their support for a magical cause. Alex and Eve's toy drive for their Secret Santa program had been such a huge success that my bet was that there wouldn't be a single child in all of Ashton Falls who would have to do without this coming Christmas morning.

"I hope you won't be needing your living room between now and Wednesday," Phyllis commented.

"I've already shooed Zak and the boys into the den with strict instructions that the living room is off limits until Alex, Eve, and I are able to make the deliveries."

"Brooklyn, Pepper, and I are available to help with deliveries as well if you need some extra hands," Phyllis offered.

"I thought Alex said Brooklyn was going home for Christmas."

"She was. She actually had an airline ticket for last Saturday, but the flight was canceled due to the storm. I offered to help her make new arrangements, but she said she was on the fence about going home anyway, and because Pepper was staying, she wanted to be here with her new family for the holiday."

I could see Phyllis was delighted by the turn of events.

"I'm sure we can use all your help. We'll meet here at the house on Wednesday morning and map out a delivery plan."

"Where should I put these cookies?" Town librarian and my grandpa's girlfriend Hazel Hampton asked after joining us.

"Just put them on the table with the other things." It seemed that pretty much everyone who'd come by to help today had brought cookies, candy, or other holiday treats. "Where's Grandpa?"

"He headed back to the den to hang out with Zak. It looks like you have a great turnout."

"And it's a good thing too. I can't believe how many toys the girls managed to collect. They worked really hard and I couldn't be prouder."

I watched as Hazel walked to the dessert table to drop off her offering. I was having the best time. Everyone was in a happy and festive mood as they wrapped gifts and talked about their own holiday plans.

The only dark spot on the perfectly wonderful day was the fact that Ellie looked sort of down. She was wrapping packages, talking, and nibbling goodies like everyone else, but her smile didn't quite reach her eyes.

I was about to pull her aside when my phone rang. "Hey, Salinger. What's up?" I greeted him.

"I just wanted to let you know that with the exception of the elusive Blugo, I've managed to track down and talk to everyone else who participated in the poker game in which Overland cheated."

"And?"

"They were all pretty mad, and a couple of the men even stated they had a plan to rough him up, but they all swore they didn't kill him. All have alibis that have been verified."

"You've been busy."

"It's my job."

"Yeah, I guess it is. Did anyone from the game know where Blugo might be or whether he was in the area at the time of the fire?"

"No one knew for sure, but they all seemed to think Blugo had moved out of that apartment building he lived in over the summer and moved into one of the summer cabins up on the mountain after the snow closed the area for the winter."

"They think he's renting a summer cabin?" I asked.

"More like squatting. After Saturday's snow the road is completely inaccessible, but I thought I might take a snowmobile up there tomorrow if I get a chance. I sort of doubt he's there, but it couldn't hurt to take a look."

"Be careful," I cautioned. "From what everyone says the guy is dangerous."

"Your concern is touching," Salinger replied with a note of sarcasm in his voice.

"I just got you broken in," I teased. "I wouldn't want to have to start over from scratch."

Salinger laughed.

"Seriously, though, be careful, and call me when you get back."

"Will do."

I headed back into the living room, where Ellie was refilling the snack trays. When she headed to the kitchen with the empty punch bowl in her hand, I knew it was my chance to check in with her.

"Hey," I said as I entered the room.

"Do you have any more lime soda?"

"In the pantry. Hang on, I'll get it. Seems like everyone is having fun."

"Yeah. It's a good turnout. When I first showed up I thought you were going to have way too many helpers and then I saw the pile of gifts the girls collected. It's really amazing."

"Yeah, they did a great job."

I handed her the soda and Ellie began mixing the punch.

"Is something wrong?" I asked.

"Does it show?"

"Only to me. Best friends have a keen eye for these types of things. I'm sure everyone else believes you're having the wonderful time you're trying to portray."

"There is something wrong, but I'm not sure this is the time or place to get into it."

"I bet the dogs need to go out. What do you say we refill the punch and then go for a walk?" I suggested.

"Yeah, okay. I could use some fresh air."

We refilled both the punch and the coffee and I announced to everyone that Ellie and I were going to take the dogs out for a bathroom break. It was cold and overcast, but the snow had temporarily stopped, allowing us to navigate the path Zak had plowed for just this purpose.

"So what's going on?" I asked.

"Levi and I have decided to split up."

I stopped walking and looked at Ellie. "Really? Why?"

"We had a long talk yesterday and we both agreed that while we love each other very much and fully intend to stay best friends, we want different things out of life. If you think about it, this split has been coming for quite a while."

"Yeah, I guess so," I admitted. "Are you okay?"

"Actually, I am. I'm feeling a little melancholy, but I've thought about it a lot, and in the end, this is the best decision. If I gave up my dream of having a family in order to remain in a relationship with Levi, I would grow to resent him, and if he agreed to having children he really doesn't want in order to remain in a relationship with me, he would grow to resent me. We decided our friendship is too precious to risk. I'm sure there will be an adjustment period for both of us, but I really think we can return to best friend status without too much damage to that relationship."

I hugged Ellie. I knew this had to be harder on her than she was letting on, but I had to agree it was the right decision.

"Can I do anything?" I asked.

"Not really. Right now I feel sort of numb, but I'm sure there's a good rant in my future, so I guess I'll need a sympathetic ear when the time comes."

"Absolutely. Day or night, I'm your girl."

"Thanks, Zoe. I feel like I've been tossed into a dark abyss of uncertainty between losing the restaurant and my split with Levi. But I also feel a spark of hope. Maybe once everything old has been stripped away, there'll be room in my life for something new and wonderful."

"I'm sure you're right." I looked toward the beach, where the dogs were chasing one another back and forth. It must be nice to be a dog, to have every day be a good one. "Have you decided what you're going to do about the restaurant?"

"Actually, I have. I talked it over with Zak and he's going to help me settle the insurance claim and pay off my loan. He's also going to handle the sale of the land so that I'll have a little cash to tide me over."

"Have you thought at all about what you want to do next?" I asked as Charlie trotted over and sat down next to me.

"I have. I'm going to work for you."

"Me? You want a job at the Zoo?"

Ellie laughed. "No, silly. Zak offered me a job at Zimmerman Academy."

"You're going to be a teacher?"

"No. I'm going to run the kitchen. You don't actually have a kitchen right now in the temporary facility, but once you open the new campus in the fall you'll need a full-time kitchen staff. And when you begin taking boarders you'll need an even larger staff."

"That's great." I hugged Ellie again. "Although I'm a little surprised Zak didn't mention he was planning to offer you a job to me."

"I don't think he did plan to. We were discussing the sale of the property and we got to talking about the future. I mentioned that I liked to cook but didn't want the responsibility that comes with owning my own business, and he suggested I work for the Academy. It wasn't something he'd thought about; it just sort of popped out. I told him I wanted to think about it and I asked him not to mention it to anyone until I decided. And I hadn't decided for sure until I was thinking things over last night, after Levi left. I decided that the job would be perfect for me. I'd have quite a bit of control over the kitchen as the manager, but I'd also have a staff, which would allow me to work a more regular schedule."

"I really do think it's perfect," I agreed. "And I'm glad my brilliant husband thought of it."

Ellie picked up a stick that was poking out of the snow and threw it down the beach for the dogs to chase. "I'm looking forward to joining the Zimmerman Academy staff. The people you've pulled together are all not only brilliant but supernice and supportive. I really think you're building a family, and I find with all the change that I'm looking forward to being part of that family."

I hugged Ellie. "You'll always be my family."

"I know. And you'll always be mine."

"Have you told your mom you aren't reopening the restaurant?" I asked.

"I have. It turns out she's thinking about selling Rosie's as well."

I frowned. "Why? She's owned Rosie's forever."

"It seems my mom's friend has been asking her to move in with her now that her husband has passed. She lives in a huge house on a large piece of land, so there's plenty of room for both of them. My mom said she's getting sick of dealing with the snow, so moving to a milder climate might be exactly what she needs. Plus, I think she's just tired. She's been working really hard for a really long time. If she moves in with her friend she can relax a bit."

I supposed Ellie had a point. Now that she was settled and out on her own, maybe it was time for Rosie to focus on herself.

Chapter 10

"What a day," I said to Zak as we snuggled on the sofa in front of the fire and shared a bottle of wine. Alex had gone home with Phyllis and the girls and Scooter had gone to a slumber party for a friend who was having a birthday, so it was just Zak and me and Pi, who was in his room working on his computer.

"It was a lot of work, but I think Alex's project is going to bring a smile to a lot of faces on Christmas morning."

"Yeah," I agreed as I stared at the lights on the tree. "She's worked so hard, and so has Eve. I think they might have started an annual event."

Zak took a sip of his wine. "Ashton Falls is a great town whose citizens take care of their own, but I really think we needed something like this."

"I agree. It was a fantastic idea. Didn't it start out as something they were doing for Zimmerman Academy?"

"A community service project. We're encouraging all the kids to do one, although we haven't made it mandatory, so some students are doing projects and some aren't. Once we get the permanent campus and have the kids full-time, I think we're going to make it part of the curriculum. Speaking of the Academy, I wanted to talk to you about something."

"You offered Ellie a job."

"Yes, I did. I didn't mean to make a decision like that without talking to you about it first, but it sort of slipped out during a conversation we were having about the restaurant and her future."

I lay my head on Zak's shoulder. "You don't have to ask my permission to hire people. It's your school, which you're paying for with your money. You can do whatever you want."

Zak turned and looked at me. "First of all, it's *our* school that we're paying for with *our* money so that *our* children will have a place to gain a quality education without us having to move. I *want* us to discuss the important decisions that need to be made. More importantly, I should have asked you before offering Ellie a job because she's your best friend. I should have made sure you were okay with her working with us before I brought it up."

"I'm fine with it. I'm more than fine with it. I think it will be the perfect job for Ellie and I think she'll be an asset to the

Academy. And I think she needs something positive to focus on, now that she and Levi have ended things."

"Good. I was hoping you would feel that way. I was sorry to hear about the breakup, but I think it's for the best."

"Yeah, me too. Wait. You heard about the breakup?" I hadn't had a chance to mention my conversation with Ellie to Zak yet.

"Yeah," Zak admitted. "Levi told me. We actually had a long talk while we were driving around rescuing people during the blizzard. He mentioned that he'd been thinking things over and he'd come to the conclusion that it would be best to end things with Ellie. He told me he planned to break the news to her the next day."

"You've known for two days that Levi planned to end things with Ellie and you didn't tell me?"

"Levi asked me not to say anything to you until he had a chance to talk to Ellie."

I supposed I understood that. I would have had a hard time not filling Ellie in, and it wouldn't have been my place to do so.

"So is that why he's been acting like such a spaz lately?" I asked.

"Partly."

"Care to elaborate?"

Zak took a deep breath. "I'm not sure how much I should say. Levi is my friend and he confided in me, but yeah, part of what Levi has been dealing with lately is the decision he knew he needed to make regarding Ellie. He loves Ellie and he didn't want to hurt her, but he could see that in the long run things weren't going to work out between them."

Zak was repeating himself. Based on his guarded expression, there had to be more going on. Something Levi would confide to Zak but didn't want me to know.

"Levi has another woman!" I blurted out. The look of surprise in Zak's eyes confirmed my suspicion. "How could he do that to Ellie?"

"He hasn't actually done anything to Ellie," Zak defended him. "But Levi did share that he'd struck up a friendship with one of the other teachers at the high school, and that the two of them had gone out for drinks a few times in a strictly platonic manner. I had the feeling that once he wrapped things up with Ellie he was interested in pursuing that relationship, but I also believed him when he assured me that nothing physical had occurred between them prior to our discussion."

"He was with her that day," I realized, "when no one could find him."

"They went skiing. He claims he forgot about the Santa booth and he didn't get your calls until later that evening because he left his phone at home."

I frowned. I sort of doubted the whole thing. Levi was pretty attached to his phone and was rarely without it. Chances were he just didn't want to deal with his responsibilities, so he'd intentionally ignored my calls.

"Ellie is going to be devastated if Levi hooks up with someone else so soon after their breakup," I pointed out.

"I know. He knows. He's decided to fly to the East Coast to spend the Christmas break with his family. He's promised me that he'll take Ellie's feelings into account before he moves ahead with a new relationship. Levi really cares for Ellie. I think he'll do as he said."

"Yeah." I had to agree with Zak. Levi did care for Ellie. He wouldn't intentionally hurt her. "I guess you're right. And I think it's a good thing he's going out of town for the holidays. It will give Ellie some space to heal. I know in my heart that splitting up is the right thing to do for both of them, but they're my best friends, so I can't help but ache for them."

"Ellie is a strong woman. She knows what she wants and she intends to get it," Zak reminded me. "It might be tough for a few months, but she'll move on with her life and hopefully we can all go back to being friends."

"I hope so."

Zak put his arm around me and gave my shoulder a squeeze. "So are you okay with all of this?"

I fought the feeling of dread deep within my soul. "Yeah. I'm okay."

"So back to what I actually wanted to talk to you about," Zak continued.

"It wasn't the fact that you hired Ellie?"

"Actually, no."

"Oh." I frowned. Zak had a tone in his voice that hinted that his news wouldn't be good.

"I'm afraid we're losing Will Danner."

"Why?"

Will was the math teacher at Zimmerman Academy. We'd just hired him over the summer and he seemed to be fitting in perfectly. The kids loved him, the staff loved him; I couldn't imagine what could have happened.

"It seems his father is getting on in years and Will feels he won't have all that much time left with him. They hadn't been all that close as of late and he wanted a chance to spend time with him while he could."

"I guess that makes sense. I'd do the same thing if I were in his shoes. Where does his father live?"

"Florida. He told me he applied for a job at the university near where his father lives at about the same time he applied to work for us. He never heard back from them, so he took the job we offered him. Then, out of the blue, he received a call from the university offering him a job a few days ago. When they first called him with the news he assumed the job was for next school year, but they wanted him right away. He hates to leave us in the lurch, but the job was too perfect to pass up."

"Does Phyllis know?" Will and Phyllis had been dating, and it seemed to me they'd been getting kind of serious.

"No. He wanted to wait until after Christmas to tell her. He felt I should know right away because he'll be leaving right after the new year and we'll need to find someone to replace him. He figured the right thing to do was to give me as much notice as possible, but he did request I not say anything to anyone else, including Phyllis."

Suddenly I wished this was news Zak hadn't shared with me. I was going to be seeing Phyllis several times over the next few days and I wasn't good at keeping secrets.

"Do you know what you're going to do about replacing him?" I asked.

"I have a few people in mind for the job," Zak answered, "though I haven't had a chance to speak to any of them yet. I can fill in myself for the short term, but I do hope to have someone in place before our trip."

"What trip?"

"That's the next thing I wanted to talk to you about."

Seemed Zak was full of surprises tonight.

"We've been invited to a murder mystery weekend in February."

I grinned. "That sounds awesome."

"So you're interested in attending?"

"Heck yeah. Where is it?"

"Ireland."

"Ireland, the country that's halfway around the world?" I clarified.

"That would be the one. Do you remember Piper Belmont?"

"The woman we met on our honeymoon?"

"Yes. She contacted me through my business e-mail, which I'd given to her husband Charles. She remembered that you were fascinated by the idea of visiting a haunted castle and managed to finagle us an invite to an event she's attending over Valentine's weekend."

"Get out! The murder mystery is being held in a haunted castle?"

"It is."

"This just keeps getting better and better." I paused. "What about the Academy?"

"Phyllis can handle things while we're gone."

"What about the kids?"

Zak adjusted his position on the sofa. He turned his body so he was looking directly at me. "My first thought was to ask Ellie to stay with them, but then I wondered if maybe we should revisit the idea of hiring some help."

"Like a nanny?"

"No. Not a nanny exactly. I think the kids are too old for that. But it would be nice to have someone who can help out with the errands and housework and can be here when we aren't."

"Like a maid?"

"No, not exactly like a maid either. I was thinking of an assistant of some sort.

Of course it would need to be someone we both liked and the kids were comfortable with. Maybe someone a little older, so there wouldn't be any territory issues with Pi. We don't have to make any decisions right away. I'm sure we can find someone to stay at the house with the kids while we're away. I just wanted you to start thinking about a more permanent solution."

"Okay. I'll think about it."

I turned to watch Pi as he walked into the room, thereby pausing the discussion.

"Jeremy and some of the guys are going to get together to jam. I thought I might join them. He's coming to pick me up. I'm going to crash at Duke's, so I guess I'll see you tomorrow."

I smiled at Zak. Were we actually going to be alone in the house? It had been forever.

"Sounds good," Zak answered. "Have fun and we'll see you tomorrow."

He turned to look at me after Pi left. "It looks like Santa just granted my Christmas wish."

I grinned back. "So how exactly should we spend our evening alone?"

Zak sat back as if considering my question. "How about we start with a swim in our heated pool and take it from there?"

I wrapped my arms around Zak's neck. "Should I get our swimsuits?"

Zak found my lips with his. "I'm thinking no."

I groaned as I leaned into Zak's body. "I'm thinking no as well."

Chapter 11

Wednesday, December 23

Both Ellie and Phyllis volunteered to help with the Secret Santa deliveries, so we decided to divide and conquer. Alex was with me, Pepper joined Ellie, and Phyllis and Eve paired together. We divided the number of stops into thirds and began loading the three vehicles with wrapped gifts, food hampers, and gift cards. Alex and Eve had called ahead and gotten delivery instructions for each residence, which were neatly typed out and distributed to each team. We all agreed to meet in town at one o'clock for lunch so we could regroup and redistribute some of the deliveries if necessary.

"This is really fun," Alex said as we pulled up to the Anderson house. The Andersons had four children, so there were a lot of gifts to drop off. Mrs. Anderson had arranged to take her children into town for a few hours so we could leave the wrapped packages without being detected; she wanted to be able to tell her children the gifts were from the real Santa.

"I'm having the best time," I agreed. "Giving back to others really does a lot for one's holiday spirit."

Alex looked down at the instructions sheet. "Mrs. Anderson left a key under the blue planter on the left side of the porch. She said we should leave the gifts in the last room on the right once we're in the hallway. The door locks, so she wants us to pull it closed behind us. We can just leave the house key in that room as well."

The Anderson family lived in a fairly large house in a nice neighborhood. They'd fallen on hard times financially when Mr. Anderson lost his job over the summer. He was currently working in a town four hours away and was only able to come home on weekends. The Andersons were trying to regain their financial footing, but Mrs. Anderson confessed that her four children most likely wouldn't have had much of a holiday if not for Secret Santa.

After we delivered all the gifts that had been set aside for the Anderson family we continued down the list. Next up was Rina Bolder and her three children. Rina's husband had passed away after a long illness the previous winter and she was working several jobs in an effort to make ends meet. Rina was at work that day, so she'd instructed us to leave the gifts in her detached garage. She'd left the side door unlocked and a blanket for us to toss over the pile should one of her older kids come looking.

Alex and I continued our mission, going from house to house until it was time to meet the others for lunch. We'd decided to meet at Rosie's, which was bittersweet now that I knew she planned to sell the restaurant. Rosie's had been around longer than I had been alive, and it would seem odd if the new owner opted to change the name, menu, or interior.

The scent of cinnamon, apple, and pumpkin greeted me as we walked in. Rosie's staff must be making pies. One of the best things about the restaurant were the pies and other pastries, which were baked fresh each day. Rosie tried to offer as many seasonal choices as she could, so the menu for the baked goods tended to change every day.

Christmas carols played softly, adding a festive atmosphere to the busy restaurant. Alex and I took a minute to watch the progress of the miniature train Rosie set up every year during the holidays. Ellie's mother really had a knack for creating a cozy environment. I just hoped the new owner would adhere to the rustic charm the popular café was famous for.

Alex and I stopped to hang an ornament on the tree that towered two stories high next to the floor-to-ceiling rock fireplace. It was a custom at Rosie's for customers to leave ornaments, which were displayed from one year to the next. By this point the giant tree was heavy with ornaments from years gone by, but visitors took great joy in trying to locate the offerings they'd left during Christmases past. I had to wonder if Rosie would leave the ornaments behind for the new owner to display or if she would choose to take them with her. I had quite a few ornaments on the tree myself, but given the fact that the others were waiting, I didn't stop to try to locate them.

"What a fun yet exhausting morning," Phyllis commented as I slid into the booth next to her.

"We're almost two thirds finished," Eve said.

"That's wonderful," I commented. "Alex and I only have about half of our deliveries completed."

"We have less than that," Ellie chimed in. "Elizabeth Proctor was home when we dropped the gifts by for the twins, and

Beth and Pepper had to talk about each and every package."

"She asked me about the gifts," Pepper defended herself.

I knew Beth was almost as boisterous and outgoing as Pepper. I imagined Ellie had had her hands full getting Pepper back on track.

"We can take a few of your deliveries," Eve offered Ellie. "So far we've had really easy ones to empty homes with easy access."

"It might be a good idea to redistribute things a bit so we can get the deliveries finished within the time frame we gave the recipients," I agreed.

"We'll just need to be sure to transfer all the packages with the correct names," Eve reminded us.

I was about to comment when my phone rang. I looked at the caller ID and saw the call was from the sheriff's office. I slid out of the booth to take the call outside.

"Hey, Salinger," I said.

"It's not Salinger. It's Janice."

"Oh, hey, sorry," I apologized to the sheriff's secretary. "I just assumed it was Salinger when I saw the number. He said he'd call me today."

"Has he?" Janice asked. "Called you?"

"Not yet. Why?"

"He took off on his snowmobile yesterday afternoon and I haven't seen or heard from him since. It's not like him not to check in if he isn't coming into the office."

My heart started to pound. Janice was right. It wasn't at all like Salinger to go off the grid. I hoped he was okay.

"He told me he was going to snowmobile up to the summer cabins to see if Blugo was hiding out up there," I explained. "That's what he was supposed to call me about. In fact, I thought he was going to call when he got back yesterday, but I sort of forgot about it. There's a lot going on this week."

"I'm really worried about him," Janice answered. "Should I call down to the county office?"

Salinger would be mad if he wasn't actually in any danger and we called his arch rival at the Bryton Lake office for no reason.

"Zak and I will take a ride up to the cabins to see if we can pick up his trail. Maybe he got stuck or something. I'll call you when we get back, and if he's still missing then, yeah, you should call the county office."

When I returned to the table I explained the situation. It was decided that all the remaining deliveries would be divided in half and Alex would join Ellie's group. I called Zak and told him about Salinger's disappearance and he agreed to get our own snowmobiles fueled and warmed up while I finished my lunch and made the trip home.

The snow had settled and the sky was blue, so the trip out to the old cabin road was actually fun and relaxing. Zak and I had decided that if Blugo was squatting in one of the cabins, and Salinger had managed to get himself into a sticky situation by going after him, we didn't want to announce our own arrival by roaring too close to the cabins with the powerful machines, so our plan was to snowmobile partway in and then continue via snowshoe.

I'd been so busy that I hadn't been out for a good snowshoe for quite a while, so I found that, despite the reason for the outing, I was looking forward to it. Besides, any alone time with Zak these days was something to cherish.

We didn't speak as we drove the snowmobiles through the deserted forest. The fresh powder made for a challenging course, but Zak and I were both experienced with the machines we drove. The fresh white snow set against the blue of the sky was breathtaking. Throw in snow-covered trees and the lake in the distance and you had a winter scene worthy of the cover of a greeting card.

Zak pulled his machine into the trees when we were about a mile from the tract of summer cabins. We'd decided this was a good place to hide the snowmobiles while we continued on foot. We had both dressed in insolating layers and the air was still, so as long as we weren't stuck out in the elements after the sun went down, we should be able to retain our body heat.

"What a gorgeous day," I stated as we began our trek toward the cabins.

"It really is. If we weren't tracking down a killer it would have been fun to bring the dogs. I feel like we've been so busy lately that all we've managed are short walks near the house."

"Maybe we can take a day hike after Christmas," I suggested. "Hopefully things will slow down a bit. Between the Secret Santa project, baking, shopping, wrapping, and everything else, we've both been really busy. By the way, did you ever find that computer you were trying to locate for Pi's gift?"

"I located it, upgraded it, and wrapped it. It's under the tree next to Scooter's skis and Tucker's bike. What did you decide to get for Alex?"

"I bought her a bunch of clothes, which she said she wanted, but I really want to find something else. Something personal. I just haven't decided what yet. Any suggestions?"

Zak continued on silently. I supposed he must be considering my question. Alex was tough. She never really asked for anything like the other two.

"I have to admit that nothing is coming to me off the top of my head, but let me think about it a bit. Did you invite Jeremy to dinner on Christmas Day?"

"I did, as well as Phyllis and the girls and Ellie and Levi, but I guess Levi won't be with us if he's decided to visit his family for the holidays. What time did Coop say he'd be here with my parents?"

Zak had sent his pilot to fetch my family from Switzerland and they were due to arrive sometime that day.

"They should be here around dinnertime. I set up a tree in their house and strung some lights around the windows."

"That's so sweet of you. I'm sure they'll appreciate it."

Zak paused at the top of an incline and looked off into the distance. He pointed toward the horizon. "Looks like smoke."

I followed Zak's finger with my eyes. "Maybe that cabin at the end of the road."

"Let's circle around behind. If we approach through the meadow Blugo, or whoever is in residence, is sure to see us."

Zak and I continued to walk around the perimeter of the complex of cabins. The deep powder made it a strenuous trip, but we were both in good shape physically, making it doable. I knew that approaching from the rear of the tract was going to add half hour at least to our trip, but Zak was right; we couldn't risk being seen from the road.

We decided we shouldn't talk as we got closer to the cabins, lest our voices carry through the canyon and give our location away. We walked single file with Zak in the lead, making the trek easier for me by quite a bit. Walking behind Zak in silence gave me time for quiet reflection. It had been such a busy month; I felt like I'd barely had a moment to stop and breath.

Christmas had always been my favorite time of year. Dad and I and Grandpa would spend a quiet morning together, followed by skiing most years. As the only child of a single parent, I'd missed out on big celebrations, but now the home I shared with Zak was filled with the family we'd built and those quiet mornings had given way to noise and a busy energy that I found I rather liked.

I wondered what it would be like when we added our own children to the mix. Would a baby add to or detract from that which we had already created? I found that I spent quite a lot of time thinking about these things lately. I knew Zak was ready for a tiny Zimmerman, but was I? I loved Zak and wanted to give him everything he desired, but something, I realized, was holding me back.

I almost ran into Zak's back when he stopped walking. "Luckily, the occupied cabin backs up to the trees," he whispered. "We'll work our way around and come in from behind. We can look in that little window on the side. Maybe we can figure out exactly what the situation is before we get too close."

"What are we going to do if Blugo is inside? What if he's holding Salinger captive? Are we just going to knock on the door and pretend to be lost?"

Zak smiled at my attempt at humor.

"We'll suss out the situation and then retreat to discuss a plan."

I followed Zak closely as he carried out the plan he'd just outlined. The window was too high for me to look through, but once he took a peek inside he motioned for me to follow him back into the woods.

"So?" I asked when we were far enough away.

"Salinger is inside. He's lying on the bed. He isn't moving."

"He isn't dead?"

"I honestly don't know. I didn't see anyone else inside. Of course someone could have been out of my line of sight. We're going to need to approach cautiously."

"I wish we had a gun," I commented.

"We do have a gun."

"We do?"

"I grabbed the tranquilizer gun you use when you need to capture injured wildlife. If it can take down a bear it should be able to take down a grown man if we need to."

Suddenly I felt a little better.

I followed Zak as we made our way back down to the cabin. He looked through the window again, then motioned for me to follow him around to the front of the cabin, where he looked in another window. Still no sign of Blugo. Zak slowly opened the door and we slipped inside. The room was warm, so it probably had been recently occupied, but now it seemed to be deserted.

I hurried over to Salinger. He was out cold but very much alive. It looked like he'd suffered a head injury, which someone had wrapped. Maybe Blugo hadn't tried to kill him. Why would you hit a man over the head and then bandage it?

"I see the cavalry has arrived," a voice said from behind us.

I turned and locked eyes with a giant of a man dressed in fur-lined clothing, holding a black bag and a bow and arrow.

"Blugo?"

"Can I ask why you're trespassing on my property?"

"We came for the sheriff. We knocked," I lied, "but you didn't answer."

He held up the black bag. "I've been out hunting for my dinner."

"I see. What happened to Salinger?" I asked.

"Hit a tree with that snowmobile of his. The man is lucky I found him. He'd have frozen to death otherwise."

"I see. Has he regained consciousness?"

"He's in and out."

"We need to get him to a hospital," I said.

"I couldn't agree more, but he ain't walking out of here and I don't have a sled."

Neither did we. I knew Levi had a sled for his snowmobile, so I headed outside and looked for a spot where the cell service worked. I had to climb a hill, but eventually I found a weak signal. Fortunately, Levi picked up and promised to meet us at the house as soon as he could get there.

"Levi is on his way with a sled," I informed Zak and Blugo when I got back inside.

I figured it would take Levi a good forty minutes to reach the cabin even if he drove his truck to the end of the plowed road and snowmobiled in. Add some time to load his snowmobile and sled onto the trailer and we were looking at an hour minimum. Plenty of time to figure out a way to ask Blugo about Jason without making him mad, because one look at the guy and I was certain this bear of a man wasn't someone to trifle with.

"So now that you've got a rescue on the way, perhaps you can tell me why you're all out here disturbing my solitude."

"We came out to look for Salinger because he hadn't returned to town as planned, and I believe the sheriff was here to talk to you about Jason Overland."

"And why would the sheriff want to talk to me about that cheating SOB?"

"He's dead. Someone murdered him."

Blugo smiled. It was a sinister-looking smile, but a smile nonetheless. "I can't tell you what a relief that is."

"A relief?"

"It took every bit of self-control I possessed not to strangle the man with my bare hands."

I stood perfectly still, unable to decide how to proceed.

"You ever had an itch you know you shouldn't scratch but you realize it's only a matter of time until you give in to the urge?" Blugo asked.

I looked at Zak. He shrugged.

"Can you elaborate?" I asked.

"After I realized Jason cheated me, I wanted to kill him. I wanted to kill him real bad. The court mandated that I take anger management classes after the last guy I put in the hospital. Figured it was a waste of time, but much to my surprise, the techniques they taught me actually worked. When I realized I was becoming obsessed with the idea of making the guy pay for his disrespect, I decided to come out here, where the temptation to skin the guy alive was a little less intense."

"So you didn't kill him?" I asked.

"No, I didn't."

"Do you know who did?"

"My guess is one of the other guys he cheated. Or maybe one of the women he used for a punching bag. If you ask me there are any number of possibilities."

Great. It looked like we were back to square one. Salinger had already talked to all the other men who'd participated in the poker game in which Jason had cheated Blugo. Of course there could have been other games and other men...

As for the women Jason had slapped around and cheated on, we'd eliminated the ones we knew about. Except one.

Chapter 12

As soon as Levi arrived with the sled, we loaded Salinger and made our way back toward his truck. We carefully placed the sheriff in the backseat and then I drove him to the hospital, while Zak and Levi took our snowmobiles home. After I'd filled Dr. Westlake in on everything I knew, I called Janice and then settled in to wait.

Salinger had woken up during the drive into town. He didn't remember what had happened to him and he didn't seem to understand that more than a day had passed since he'd set out on his snowmobile. He said everything was fuzzy, which I could totally understand because the same thing had happened to me when I'd been hit in the head.

I used the time I had while I was sitting in the hospital waiting for news about Salinger to go over my suspect list one more time.

Tina had suggested that the killer could be Riley, but she had an alibi.

Riley had suggested that the killer could be Andrew Dover, Kelly Arlington, Bram Willard, Tina Littleton, or Blugo.

Bram had said he'd been working and provided several of his clerks as his alibi, although I hadn't actually spoken to those employees. Still, my gut told me Bram wasn't our guy.

Andrew told me he was skiing on the day Jason was killed. Again, I hadn't actually spoken to his witnesses, but likewise I had a feeling he wasn't the killer.

Blugo claimed not to have killed Jason, but he'd been alone when Jason died and didn't seem to have an alibi. He could have killed Salinger but had taken care of him instead. His story seemed sincere, so in my mind he'd moved to the bottom of the suspect list.

As for Kelly, she very well could have woken up and stabbed Jason, but the more I thought about it, the more certain I was that I'd seen another person come into the restaurant that day. I still didn't have a face to go with the blurry image, but the feeling that it was real and not just a trick of the light was becoming stronger as time went by.

I thought about the fifth name Riley had given me: Tina Littleton. She'd admitted to having an affair with Jason and that he'd broken things off with her. She'd also admitted to stalking Riley, but that was where things began to fall apart. She'd told me that Riley was possessive, but after speaking to the woman herself, I had the impression she was the complete opposite. She seemed to view her relationship with Jason as nothing more than a way to pass the time. Tina also had told me that she was over Jason and therefore no longer stalking Riley, but she'd also said she'd seen Jason and Riley together at Lucky's on the day of the fire. She didn't seem the type to hang out in a seedy bar on her own for recreational purposes, so what was she doing there? Perhaps she hadn't given up her stalking after all. Could she have followed Jason to Ellie's Beach Hut after he left the bar?

And then there was the fact that the first time I'd spoken to Tina, she'd mentioned that Riley was exactly the type to stick a knife into some guy's back if he strayed. At that point it wasn't public knowledge that Jason had been stabbed, let alone in the back. Could she, in an attempt to cast suspicion on Riley, have inadvertently provided a fact that only the killer would know?

I took out my phone to call Zak just as Dr. Westlake entered the waiting room.

"So?" I asked.

"The sheriff's going to be fine. I'm going to keep him for a day or two, just to make sure the head wound isn't more serious than it appears, but he should make a full recovery."

I let out the breath I'd been subconsciously holding ever since I'd dropped Salinger off. "That's good."

Dr. Westlake and I spoke for a few more minutes and then I called Janice to give her the good news. By the time I completed my call Zak had joined me in the waiting room.

"He's going to be fine," I shared.

"That's good."

"Where's Levi?"

"On his way to the airport for his flight east."

I'd almost forgotten about that.

"Are you ready to go home?" Zak asked.

"Almost. I want to stop off at the Christmas store first."

Zak gave me an odd look. I considered making up a lie about needing Santa napkins or something, but he'd been so great and I really did owe him the truth, so I filled him in on my theory that Tina had been the killer all along.

"You make a good argument," Zak affirmed. "Who's acting sheriff now that Salinger is in the hospital?"

"Janice said they were sending someone up from the county office. She wasn't sure who, but they should be here within the hour."

"Maybe we should wait and let Salinger's replacement handle this," Zak suggested.

I frowned.

"Of course we could always use a few more ornaments for the tree."

I smiled.

"We talk to her in a public place, but that's it. If we still think she's guilty of killing Jason we wait and let the replacement deputy handle it. Agreed?"

"Agreed."

The Christmas store was as packed as it had been every other time I'd stopped by in the past month. The lines at the front counter were long and the aisles were cluttered with merchandise that had been strewn about as hordes of customers sorted through the inventory. I couldn't help but notice Zak's eyes grow large as he viewed the sleigh replica featured in the center of the room.

"I noticed the kits for those sleighs when I've been in here before, but I thought they'd look cheesy when assembled so I passed. The finished product isn't half bad, though."

"We really don't have anywhere to store a giant sleigh," I told Zak.

"I guess you're right. When I was a kid, before I moved to Ashton Falls, my friend had a farm not far from where I lived. He had this old sleigh that had been his grandfather's, I think. Every year he'd hook a couple of his horses up to it and we'd take off through the woods. There was something kind of perfect about riding through a forest of fresh snow."

"We just did that on the snowmobiles."

"Yeah. But a sleigh is different. Not that this sleigh is going to take anyone anywhere. It just brought back a fond memory."

"We never did get to take that sleigh ride in town with the storm and all. Maybe we still can," I offered.

"Yeah, maybe."

"For now, let's talk to Tina and get out of here. It's hot with all these bodies."

Zak looked around the store. He was a tall man who was able to see over the heads of most people, and I was a short woman who wasn't able to see much of anything, so I figured having him look for Tina was our best bet.

"I don't see her."

"Maybe we can ask one of her coworkers if she's in today. It's possible she has the day off."

Zak spotted the owner of the store, shelving ornaments a row over, so we pushed our way through the crowd to ask her about Tina.

"Tina's gone."

"For the day?" I clarified.

"For good. She came in yesterday and told us she was moving out of the area. She left something for you. Hang on; I'll get it."

The store owner walked into the back and then came out a few minutes later with an envelope in her hand.

"I'm not sure what's in it, but she seemed to think you'd be by looking for her and wanted me to be sure you got this."

"Okay. Thanks."

Zak and I left the store. We headed back out to the truck and climbed inside. I opened the envelope and pulled out the letter.

Dear Zoe,

I figured it was only a matter of time until you figured out I was the one who killed Jason, so I decided to get out of town while the getting was possible. By the time you read this you'll probably have figured out that I really wasn't over Jason. That man used me. He made me love him when all the while he was using me as a pawn in some twisted game he was playing with Kelly. I hate to admit it, but his lies wormed their way into my soul and at some point my love turned into an obsession to destroy him the way he'd destroyed me.

I began stalking him, but I didn't plan to kill him. I followed him to Lucky's on the day of the fire and then hid in the background while he partied the afternoon away with Riley. She didn't love him the way I did. He should have seen that. He should have been with me.

When he left the bar I followed him to the restaurant only to find him chatting up the woman he'd sworn he was done with. I was all set to confront him when you came by. I hid in the shadows while he hit first Kelly and then you. He picked up a piece of the broken chair he'd already hit you with and was preparing to hit you again, and I picked up a knife that was sitting on the counter and stabbed him in the back. He never saw it coming.

When I left the building wasn't on fire. I swear it. You've always been nice to me and I would never have risked your life.

I won't leave a forwarding address for obvious reasons, but I hope you can find it in your heart to forgive me. You're actually one of the good ones.

Sincerely,
Tina

"Wow," I said after I finished reading the letter aloud to Zak. "I kind of feel sorry for her. And grateful. She most likely did save my life. If Jason had hit me again I might not have regained consciousness and Kelly and I would have both perished in the fire."

"What do you want to do?" Zak asked.

"I guess we could hand this over to the deputy who comes to replace Salinger and get on with our Christmas, though I suppose if we decided to wait to give it to Salinger when he recovers no one would really blame us."

"Waiting will make it harder to catch her," Zak pointed out.

"True. But she's been gone for a whole day already. It's going to be pretty hard anyway."

"How about we take it to Salinger when we visit tomorrow and let him decide?" Zak suggested.

"Sounds like a plan."

Chapter 13

Friday, December 25

I had a feeling this Christmas was going to go down in my memory as one of the best ever. The incident with the sleigh in the Christmas store had finally given me an idea of what to get for the man who had everything. I rented a horse and sleigh for two days and had it delivered the afternoon before Christmas Eve. To say that Zak was shocked would be putting it mildly. The entire Donovan-Zimmerman clan had shared a memorable evening gliding through the woods under a silver moon, singing carols while snuggled under a blanket drinking hot cocoa.

We'd even taken the sleigh into town for Christmas Eve services, and Zak and the kids had had a wonderful time providing rides for their friends.

After we got home we gathered by the fire and shared our favorite moments of the day, and then the kids went to bed and Zak and I shared our own magical Christmas Eve night.

Of course peace and serenity had given way to chaos once Christmas Day arrived.

"I think we're going to need more folding chairs," Jeremy said to me as I struggled to make room in the refrigerator for the cheesecake he'd brought to share.

"In the attic. One of the kids can show you."

"Do you have a larger pot to boil the potatoes?" Hazel asked as soon as Jeremy left to find the chairs.

"Bottom shelf in the very back of the walk-in pantry," I answered.

Zak had shopped for all the food and had prepared everything that could be done ahead of time, but once our guests arrived everyone wanted a sleigh ride, so he'd been outdoors while I was left in the kitchen. Maybe covering for him while he played with the kids was my actual Christmas gift.

"Everything looks perfect." Mom hugged me as I tried to peel carrots.

"Thanks. Zak put a lot of thought into the meal. He's been poring over cookbooks for weeks."

"I'm sure your dad can handle the sleigh if you think Zak would rather be in here preparing his feast."

I looked out the window. Zak had just pulled up with the latest group and he had the biggest grin I'd ever seen on his face. "Thanks, but I think he's having fun."

"Well, at least let me help you." Mom pulled on an apron.

"I never got the chance to talk to you about your trip. How was it?"

"It was wonderful. I love my life in Ashton Falls and wouldn't trade it for anything, but I didn't realize how much I missed my family until I walked into the chalet."

"I'm glad you had a nice time. How did Harper do with so many new faces?"

"She was great. She was a little shy the first day or two, but after that she was toddling around like she owned the place. I really want to take you and Zak there for a visit. I know you have a lot of responsibility with the kids and the new school, but maybe a short trip sometime."

I smiled. "I'd like that."

"Do you need any help?" Ellie walked in through the back door, which led out to the deck that overlooked the lake. It was a sunny day, so Zak had lit a bunch of portable fire pits so anyone who wished could stay warm while enjoying the view.

"Do I!" I answered. "Zak left a list of everything he'd planned for the meal. I'm trying to prepare things in a logical order, but I wouldn't mind the help of an actual cook."

Ellie picked up the list. She looked around the kitchen and frowned.

"That bad?" I asked.

"Not at all. Look, you've been stuck in here for most of the day. Why don't you go out and get some fresh air and I'll take over for a bit?"

Thank you, Ellie.

I untied my apron and got out before she changed her mind. I'd really wanted to take over for Zak so he could relax and enjoy himself for a while, but cooking wasn't my forte.

It was unseasonably warm, which, combined with all the fresh snow, made for a perfect day for snow sports and other outdoor activities. Zak was out on a sleigh run, so I took Charlie and the other dogs for a quick romp down the beach. When I returned Zak was speaking to a man wearing a dark jacket. Standing next to him was a little girl who looked like Tabitha, although her back was to me.

"Tabitha?" I said when I got closer.

The girl turned around and ran over to me. She put her arms around my waist and gave it a good, hard hug.

"Thank you for talking to Santa for me."

My look of confusion must have been evident so her father joined in. "When we got up this morning Cupcake was sitting under the tree waiting for us."

"She was?"

"Tabitha wanted to thank you. I wanted to thank you. I can't tell you how much having Cupcake means to both of us."

"I didn't really do anything."

"You talked to Santa, just like you said you would." Tabitha pulled my head down so she could whisper in my ear, "I knew you were the Santa in town when I came to the shelter. I didn't want to spoil my wish by saying so. I know you spoke to the real Santa about Cupcake. Thank you."

She kissed my cheek and then stepped away. I was pretty sure I was going to cry.

A few minutes later Zak had my dad take Tabitha and her dad for a sleigh ride. He claimed he was getting cold, but I thought he just wanted to speak to me in private.

"I thought you said you couldn't find the dog."

"I couldn't. I didn't. Maybe the dad found her and wanted to surprise his daughter."

"No. He said he was as surprised as she was when they came downstairs this morning and Cupcake was sitting among the gifts he'd bought."

"You don't think the real Santa...?"

Zak pulled me into his arms and kissed the tip of my cold nose. "Yes, Zoe Donovan-Zimmerman, I do think the real Santa brought some Christmas magic to a sad little girl."

Note to reader:

As you've noticed by now, I didn't include the interactive component in this book. Some people loved it and some hated it, but I realized after doing it a few times that continuing with that format would be limiting given some of the plots I have lined up.

I do like the idea of seeing the world through the eyes of the minor characters, however, so I've decided to break *Zimmerman Academy* off from the main Zoe books and publish short stories (15K–20K) during the gaps between the main books. These shorts will be offered for $.99 and will be told from differing perspectives. I'll continue to have stories told from Phyllis's perspective, but there will also be shorts told from other characters' as well.

The first *Zimmerman Academy* short I have planned is scheduled to go on sale on January 15. The book is titled: *Zimmerman Academy: The New Normal* and will be told from Ellie's perspective.

Ellie will have a mystery to solve and a new math teacher to welcome to Ashton Falls while Zoe and Zak are out of town.

I plan to publish three or four shorts in 2016.

I've included a short story in this book told from Phyllis's perspective. It takes place after this book ends. The format is different from the previous *Zimmerman Academy* shorts, the format used more closely resembling the one for the new independently published short stories. The shorts I will offer for sale will be about 4 times as long as this sample. I hope you enjoy it.

Zimmerman Academy

Something Lost, Something Found

As told from the viewpoint of Phyllis King

Chapter 1

They say sixty is the new forty. I certainly hoped that was true because I'd just spent the last four hours boxing up all my old lady clothes to make room for the new wardrobe I planned to buy when the girls and I went on our first annual post-holiday clearance shopping spree. I realize that donating 70 percent of my wardrobe is an extravagant thing to do, but the past few weeks have been an emotional roller coaster and I feel, for the first time in my life, that I want to leave my old self behind and invent something entirely new. I haven't worked out all the details yet, but I do know that the Phyllis King who will return to work at Zimmerman Academy, where I am both the principal and a teacher, will be a new and improved version of the sixty-two-year-old who went on break just under two weeks ago.

On the upside of the roller coaster, I had a wonderful Christmas with the three teenagers who now share my life: Brooklyn Banks, a gorgeous and sophisticated sixteen-year–old; Prudence Pepperton, a friendly and energetic fifteen-year-old; and Eve Lambert, a brilliant and introverted fourteen-year-old. We really did have the perfect holiday, and although we are not a real family, I feel that we have started traditions that will endure wherever our paths take us.

Having the girls in my life has given me a new perspective, as well as a renewed enthusiasm for the magic of everyday moments. Who knew how much joy could be had from simple things such as buying trinkets for stockings, singing carols as a family, or working together to create a big Christmas brunch? Prior to the arrival of the girls my holidays had been simple, solitary, and uneventful. I may be a bit late out of the gate, but I feel like Phyllis King the academic is finally blossoming into Phyllis King the woman.

On the down side of the roller coaster is the fact that the one and only man I ever felt I could love has left Ashton Falls to be with his elderly father. I cannot fault Will or his decision to do what he knew in his heart needed to be done. It is a noble man who will put the needs of his family above his own desires. Still, I find that Will has left a hollow place in my heart and an emptiness in my life that I feel an overwhelming desire to fill. The girls are doing their best to keep me distracted, thus the suggestion of the shopping trip in the first place.

"Don't look at me like that," I said to my cat, Charlotte, who was lying on my bed watching me box up the clothes I'd picked out of my closet. "I have not lost my mind. It's more that I've *changed* my mind, and these old clothes no longer fit my new paradigm."

Charlotte rolled over onto her back, a movement that indicated that she was bored with my chatter and wanted her belly rubbed.

I ignored her.

"I'd fallen into such a rut," I continued. "It's almost as if I was sleepwalking through life until the girls came along and woke me up. Not that I wasn't living a perfectly useful life. It's just that my life had become one-dimensional and I'd let it happen."

I held up a wool jacket that was half of a wool dress suit. The skirt would have to go, but the jacket might pair nicely with slacks and a sweater.

"What do you think?" I asked Charlotte.

She jumped off the bed and wandered into my closet, making it clear she really couldn't care less what I did with the jacket.

I decided to keep it to wear with the new jeans and knee-high boots the girls had talked me into buying. It was a good-quality cloth, and the neutral camel color would go with a lot of different things.

I hung up the jacket and then stood in front of the full-length mirror. I tried to be objective as I considered my image. While my hair was still the same waist-length style in which I'd worn it my entire life, the girls had talked me into getting highlights to lessen the gray. My skin was smooth and line free due to a lifetime of rigorous adherence to a moisturizing routine, and I'd managed to keep a slim figure, although lord knew it would do me good to add a toning routine to my day.

"Do you think I should join a gym?"

"Meow," Charlotte commented as she wandered back into the bedroom from the closet.

I took that as signifying agreement.

Between the highlights in my hair, the addition of makeup that Brooklyn had spent hours teaching me how to apply, and the younger and hipper-looking clothes, I really did look as if I could pass for forty, or at least forty-five. I found it hard to remember why I'd never paid any mind to my appearance in the first place.

"I'm thinking that I'll wear my new plum sweater into town. Plum is a good color on me. My mama always told me that plum brought out the sparkle in my eyes."

Charlotte jumped up onto the dresser and knocked the novel I was reading onto the floor. I was certain she was trying to remind me not to lose sight of who I was in the process of reinventing who I wanted to be. Charlotte had a point, but up to this moment I'd lived my entire life in the pursuit of academic achievement and had paid little attention to anything else. I'd never dated, fallen in love, or married. I'd never had children nor engaged in relationships or friendships that weren't related to the academic world in which I'd lived. I'd lived a useful and purposeful life and didn't necessarily regret the choices I'd made, but the opportunity to veer from the path I'd chosen and travel the one unfollowed left me feeling more alive than I had in years.

I changed into my plum sweater, which I paired with black jeans and a soft leather jacket. I picked up the first of five perfectly packed boxes and started down the hall.

"Let me help you with that," Pepper offered.

"I've got this one fine, but there are four more in my room if you want to grab one of those."

I carried the box down the stairs and set it next to the front door. My garage was in the rear of the property, but I decided I'd pull my car up to the front curb, cutting the distance needed to load the boxes in half.

The house, which two days ago had been decorated for the holiday, had been returned to its previous state of tidiness after a long day of undecorating. The tree that had stood in front of the window had been stripped of the ornaments the girls and I had purchased and had been left out on the curb for the garbage truck when it next came by.

I had especially enjoyed all the lights we'd strung: the small twinkle lights that had been added to the garland we'd wound along the banister, the festive red and green candle lights that had graced almost every tabletop, and the larger Christmas lights that had been strung around the windows at the front of the house.

"Are you going out?" I asked Pepper, who arrived with the second box. She had on boots and a jacket, indicating that she planned to venture outdoors.

"Chad is picking me up in a few minutes. We are going to a movie."

Chad Carson was a fifteen-year-old student at Zimmerman Academy and about as close to being a personality double to Pepper as you were likely to find. The two energetic extroverts had been the best of friends from the day they met.

"That sounds like fun," I responded. "What are you going to see?"

"The new action flick that just came out. I can't remember the name, but it's the one with that cutie pie actor Brooklyn is always going on and on about. You can come with us if you'd like."

"Thanks, dear, but I'm planning to head into town to run a few errands. I should be back before you return, but be sure to bring your house key just in case."

"It's in my pocket. Are you sure you don't want to come?"

"I'm sure. You kids have fun."

"Thanks. We will."

After Pepper left the house I went back upstairs for the remaining three boxes. There was a definite satisfaction that came from purging the clothes I'd spent an adulthood collecting, but I experienced a certain nostalgia as well. The sturdy, practical clothing I'd purchased along the way had served me well, even if it no longer fit the new lifestyle I was in the process of designing for myself.

I picked up the next box and headed out of my bedroom. Luckily, I ran into Brooklyn on the stairs, who offered to lend a helping hand. Brooklyn is the eldest of the three and in some ways the hardest to know. She is a perfectly lovely girl, but it is obvious that she has been hurt in the past and therefore guards her heart against future pain by maintaining a barely discernable distance between herself and everyone else.

"Are you going out as well?" I asked as we hauled the three remaining boxes down the stairs.

"Pi is coming to pick me up. He has a gig in Bryton Lake and I'm going to go with him."

Pi was one of the three Zimmerman Academy students living with Zoe and Zak Zimmerman. He was sixteen, as was Brooklyn, and the two seemed to enjoy spending time together, although I think any hope Brooklyn had of entering into a romantic relationship with the musician has gone by the wayside.

"The roads will be icy when you come home," I instructed Brooklyn. "Be sure to remind Pi to take it easy."

"I will," Brooklyn promised as she trotted out the front door.

I looked around the empty house. I knew Eve and Alex Bremmerton, another of the students living with Zak and Zoe, were around somewhere. I doubted they'd want to go into town with me, but I hated to leave without telling them where I was going. If I knew Eve and Alex, they were probably reading or working on a project, so I headed to the library.

"What are you girls working on?" I asked when I found them huddled over a table.

"A treasure map," Eve answered.

"A treasure map?"

"Before we went on break Professor Carlton gave us an extra-credit assignment. We thought it would be fun to try to solve the mystery," Eve explained.

"What mystery?"

"A year or so ago Zoe helped a man named Burton Ozwald find the treasure his grandpa left hidden for his father back in 1940," Eve answered. "All she had to go on was a letter with a riddle, so she enlisted the assistance of Professor Carlton and a few others to help her find the gold."

I did seem to remember something about that.

"Anyway, Professor Carlton thought it would be fun for those of us who had time to try to find the treasure using the same clues that were in the original letter. He hid something in the location where Zoe ended up finding the treasure and the first one to find it will receive a bunch of extra credit points."

"It does sound like fun," I admitted, "but don't you both already have straight As?"

"We do," Alex confirmed, "but the assignment sounded like fun, and a good way to learn more about local history. The thing is, we might have hit a roadblock."

"Do you want some help?" I asked. The assignment really did sound fascinating.

"We can use all the help we can get," Eve answered.

I sat down at the table with the girls.

"Here's what we know so far," Eve continued. "The original letter Burton Ozwald had was really just a riddle that led to an old masthead that was brought to Devil's Den by a man named Warren Goldberg in 1908. It seems he owned a sailing vessel at one time, which he sold to fund his journey west. This article," Eve held up an old newspaper clipping, "says that while he sold the boat to an exporter, he kept the masthead, which held special meaning for him. At some point the masthead ended up in the local bar. That building no longer exists, but during the original treasure hunt Zoe tracked it down to the storage room of the Ashton Falls Museum. Alex and I were able to follow the clues to the museum and, as Zoe had, we discovered a secret drawer. Professor Carlton hid the clue in the drawer in order to replicate the series of events that took place during the original treasure hunt."

I had to hand it to Ethan. He'd certainly gone to a lot of effort to make studying the history of Ashton Falls interesting.

"The clue in the drawer instructed us to look for the medic's seal," Alex continued. "There were a few extra clues I don't believe Zoe had access to at the time of the real treasure hunt, but we were able to track down the information we needed at the library, where a photo of the old clinic was being held for our project. On the exterior of the building was a seal with the words *legatum sit amet*, which is Latin for 'Life Is Love's Legacy.' We can't figure out where to go from there. Professor Carlton did say that Zoe found the treasure, so it seems the riddle is solvable. We just haven't been able to figure it out."

I looked down at the books and materials the girls had spread out on the table. A treasure hunt was just the thing I needed to occupy my mind.

"All right, why don't we start at the beginning?" I suggested. "What was the original clue Professor Carlton gave you?"

Eve pushed a piece of paper in front of me. It read:

To begin the quest
I give to you
A maiden's breast
As the initial clue.

"This is the clue that led to the masthead of a mermaid that had once graced a ship but at some point had been removed and attached to a bar," Eve restated. "As I indicated earlier, at some point it was removed from the bar and given to the museum. When it began to decay it was moved to the storage room, where it still is to this day. This is the clue we found in the secret drawer."

Eve pushed a second piece of paper in front of me. It read:

To find what's next
You must reveal
The hidden text
In the medic's seal.

"I understand that in the original treasure hunt this clue led to the hospital, but I guess Professor Carlton didn't want us digging around in the hospital, so he provided additional clues that led us to the library," Alex added. "A replica of the original photo that was used in the first treasure hunt was waiting for us."

"As we said, when translated the seal says 'Life Is Love's Legacy,'" Eve continued. "We don't know where to go from there."

I looked at the information the girls had gathered. It appeared as if they had followed the clues correctly, yet I wasn't able to figure out what should come next either. "I was planning to go into town to donate the clothes I have boxed up. If you want to come with me, we can stop off at the library to see if Hazel has anything else up her sleeve."

Hazel Hampton is the local librarian.

"I'm in," Alex answered.

"Me too," Eve seconded.

Chapter 2

The alpine town of Ashton Falls was busy with shoppers taking advantage of the clear, sunny day as well as the post-holiday sales. I'd planned to do the majority of my shopping at the mall in Bryton Lake, but perhaps I'd check out the local retail outlets as well.

I dropped the boxes of clothes off at the second-hand store that served as a fund-raiser for the local Food for Families program before heading to the library. Ethan's assignment had me intrigued. Although I'd heard about the outcome of the treasure hunt when it happened, I hadn't been involved and so wasn't privy to the details leading up to the end result.

"Did you girls figure out the clue already?" Hazel asked.

"Actually, the opposite." Eve shook her head.

"We figured out that the seal says 'Life Is Love's Legacy,' but we can't figure out how this will lead us to the next clue."

Hazel held out her hand, indicating that Eve should pass the photo of the old clinic to her. She pointed to the seal. "Do you notice anything else?"

The girls and I all frowned as we tried to figure out what Hazel was referring to.

"Here." Hazel handed Eve a small magnifying glass. "Look at it through this."

"'LIV,'" Eve stated. "It says 'LIV' all in caps on the bottom of the seal."

"So what does that mean?" Alex asked.

Hazel just smiled. I could see she was going to let the girls work on the answer themselves. They took the photo and a pad of paper and headed over to a nearby table. Hazel handed them a box of old clippings, telling them that the answer to the riddle could be found within that box.

"Ethan certainly has gone to a lot of trouble to teach the kids a bit of Ashton Falls' history," I commented to Hazel.

"He seems to be having fun with it, although I think Eve and Alex are the only students still working on it. Most of the Zimmerman Academy kids went home for break, and those who stayed seemed to have other plans. By the way, I was sorry to hear that we lost Will. He was a good man and an excellent teacher."

"Yes," I agreed. "He was. I'm really going to miss him."

Hazel squeezed my hand. We had similar backgrounds in that neither of us had ever married or had children of our own, despite the fact that we adored children. Hazel had been dating Zoe's grandfather, Luke Donovan, for a while now, and it seemed they were getting serious. I hoped that I'd find another man to love. Now that I'd had a taste of what it was like to feel the flutter of awakening desire, I found I rather craved it.

"I think we found it," Eve said. "'LIV' stands for the roman numeral 54." Eve held up an old newspaper clipping. "This article is entitled 'A TRIBUTE TO THE 54.' The article is from the *Chronicle*, and it's dated October 12, 1910. There's a photo of a bunch of men and a couple of women standing in front of the clinic. The article states:

> "'A year ago today fifty-four men from the small mining camp of Devil's Den pooled their meager resources to bring a doctor from our local hospital to their small village to save the life of a prostitute who had developed complications from a late-term pregnancy. Dr. Owen Ozwald, a recently hired resident at the hospital, was chosen for the task. Upon his arrival at the

camp, the doctor found admiration and affection for a community that had come together to save the life of one of their own. Dr. Ozwald was so moved by the commitment of the community to save a single life that he handed in his resignation and announced plans to move his family to Devil's Den in order to open a clinic for those who live in the area. The highly anticipated Devil's Den Medical Clinic opened today and the entire town came out for the celebration. Lilly England, the local madame, who acts as a mother of sorts to the girls, attributes the close-knit community and the willingness of its members to make sacrifices for one another with its isolation from the outside world.'"

"So Mr. Ozwald's grandfather was the local doctor," I realized.

"The thing is, I still don't know how this relates to the next clue," Alex said.

Hazel frowned. "When we got to this point in the original treasure hunt Zoe looked at the photo and made a huge leap as to where she thought the treasure might be hidden, but now that I think about it, we never did actually find the next clue. It seems there must have been one."

I was confused and I could tell by the look on the girls' faces they were as well.

"If you notice in the photo," Hazel elaborated, "the doctor has his arm around the woman on his right. Based on the way she's dressed, Zoe speculated that she was the Lilly England mentioned in the article. She also speculated that the woman on the left with the baby was the prostitute the doctor must have saved. Somehow she made a giant leap from that assumption to deciding that Dr. Ozwald must have given the treasure to Lilly for safekeeping. The next thing I knew, we were heading to the abandoned house Lilly used to live in to look for the treasure."

"Did you find it?" Eve asked.

"We did. The thing is, it never occurred to me at the time that if Owen Ozwald set up a treasure hunt for his son, he would have provided another riddle or clue relating to the seal. I doubt he would assume someone like Zoe would be the one to embark on the hunt for the treasure he left. Very few people could make the leap Zoe did and solve the riddles."

"So we might actually be able to find a clue that has never been found before if we can figure this out," Alex asserted.

"Did you bring the riddles with you?" I asked Eve.

"Yeah." She pulled a piece of paper out of her pocket.

"The first riddle led to a second one, so it makes sense that the second riddle would lead to a third."

I looked at the second riddle again.

To find what's next
You must reveal
The hidden text
In the medic's seal.

"What hidden text?" I asked. "The words *legatum sit amet*, as well as the numeral LIV, are clearly shown on the seal. They were difficult to see from the grainy photo, but at the time Dr. Ozwald planned the treasure hunt, the seal was on the building and clearly visible. There must be a hidden message somewhere on the seal that Ethan and Zoe didn't take into consideration the first time around."

"You make a good point," Hazel agreed. "Let's scan the photo of the seal into the computer; then we can enlarge it on the screen. Maybe there are words hidden somewhere else in the design."

Hazel, the girls, and I looked until we were cross-eyed, but we couldn't find any hidden letters.

"What if the hidden message is within the letters we have?" Alex suggested.

"Like a word scramble?" Hazel asked.

Alex shrugged. "It's just a thought."

"I guess it couldn't hurt to put the clue through the unscramble program I have on the computer," Hazel offered. She pulled the program up on her computer. "If you take the letters from *legatum sit amet* in their entirety, we have quite a few choices, although we don't come up with a single fourteen-letter word. There are several ten-letter words, including *stalagmite*, which fits because Devil's Den was a mining town, and a clue could very well have been left in one of the mines."

"Yeah, but which one?" Alex asked.

"What letters are left?" I wondered.

"U-M-E-T," Hazel answered.

"Mute?" Eve guessed.

"That doesn't ring a bell," I admitted. "Besides, there was no such thing as a computer or an unscramble program back then. It had to be something simpler. Maybe something to do with the translated text."

"Life is love's legacy," Eve repeated.

"Dr. Ozwald wanted to leave his son a legacy or inheritance," Hazel pointed out.

"Maybe Zoe was right all along. Maybe Dr. Ozwald simply arranged for Lilly to hide the gold and then give it to his son when he arrived. Maybe there really isn't another clue," Alex suggested.

"I don't know," Eve said. "The clue leading to the seal clearly states that we're looking for hidden text. Is there another seal?"

"Zoe got the photo we have from Dr. Westlake," Hazel informed us. "She did say he had a whole box of old documents."

"I guess it couldn't hurt to ask him if we can take a look," I suggested.

"Yes, let's." Alex jumped up.

"Maybe we should call Dr. Carlton to fill him in on our plan," I said. "If there is another clue I'm sure he would want to be in on the finding."

Both girls agreed immediately.

I called Ethan, who was, as I suspected, intrigued by our line of thinking. He agreed to meet us at the hospital. Once I'd arranged a place for us to meet, the girls and I thanked Hazel and then headed to the hospital. Luckily, Dr. Westlake was in and agreed to our looking through the boxes of old records and photographs from the clinic at the mining camp.

It turned out there was quite a lot of material to go through, so it was a good two hours before anyone found anything of relevance.

"Look at this." Alex held up an unopened letter that had been closed with a wax seal.

"Who's it made out to?" I asked.

"No one. The envelope is blank. What I found interesting is the seal on the back."

I took the envelope from Alex. The wax seal had the letter *O* in the middle, but what was really interesting was the small words that were so tiny as to be unnoticeable around the outside edge.

"I'm afraid my old eyes can't make out such small type." I handed the envelope back to Alex.

"It says, 'Seek to know for whom the bell tolls,'" Alex informed me.

"The *O* on the seal could stand for Ozwald," Eve said, excitement in her voice. "Maybe this is the seal that was referred to in the letter. Maybe Dr. Ozwald wanted his son to go to a place in town with a bell. Do we have any idea where that might be?"

"The schoolhouse," I suggested.

"Is the schoolhouse still here?" Alex asked.

"I'm afraid not," I answered.

"Phyllis is correct; the old school building has been gone for years," Ethan confirmed. "But the bell that hung in the tower is still around. It's hanging in the bell tower of the church."

"Do you think that bell somehow holds the missing clue?" Eve asked.

"There's only one way to find out," Ethan answered.

We packed everything up and returned it to Dr. Westlake, then headed to the Ashton Falls Community Church. Pastor Dan was fine with our climbing up into the tower to look at the old bell. Engraved on the side of the bell was one word: *Lilly*. It appeared we'd found the missing clue at last.

Recipes for *Santa Sleuth*

Baked Rice—submitted by Vivian Shane
Sweet Potato Soufflé—submitted by Teresa Kander
Crock-Pot Turkey Breast Roast—submitted by Marie Rice
Punch Bowl Cake—submitted by Wanda Downs
Peanut Butter Cookies—submitted by Elaine Robinson
Mexican Wedding Bells—submitted by Pam Curran
Santa Whiskers—submitted by Nancy Farris
Almond Banket—submitted by Joanne Kocourek
Festive Fudge—submitted by Kathleen Kaminski
Peanut Brittle—submitted by Vivian Shane
Divinity—submitted by Pam Curran
Yorkshire Pudding—submitted by Janel Flynn

Baked Rice

Submitted by Vivian Shane

This recipe has been passed down through the generations in my family. I've submitted it in its original form, with the so-very-specific instructions on how my grandmother cooked the rice—too funny!

Cook 1 cup rice until tender (1 cup to 1½ cup water—bring to a boil uncovered at medium, turn to low, and put lid on partway; when holes appear in rice mixture, turn to simmer and put cover on and cook for 15 minutes).

Mix together 3 beaten eggs, ½ cup sugar, ½ cup cream, ½ cup raisins, and 1 tsp. vanilla.

Sprinkle with cinnamon.

Bake at 350 degrees for 30 minutes or until custard is set. Great with baked ham or even as dessert!

Sweet Potato Soufflé

Submitted by Teresa Kander

This is a recipe I started making for the holidays from the time I was living on my own, about thirty years ago. It was requested by extended family members at my grandmother's every year, and I continue to make it for nuclear family holiday dinners.

4 cups mashed sweet potatoes
1 cup sugar
2 eggs
½ cup milk
½ tsp. salt
⅓ stick butter or margarine (melted)
1 tsp. vanilla

Mix well. Pour into buttered pan.

Topping:
1 cup brown sugar
½ cup flour
⅓ cup butter or margarine (melted)
1 cup pecans

Crumble topping evenly over potato mixture. Bake at 350 degrees for 35–45 minutes uncovered.

Crock-Pot Turkey Breast Roast

Submitted by Marie Rice

It was a happy accident that I discovered this recipe. The first Thanksgiving when none of our children would be in town, it was just the two of us for Thanksgiving dinner. Hubby loves turkey at the holidays, but I didn't want to do the traditional big bird in the oven. I picked up a couple of three-pound turkey breast roasts at the grocery store. I'd seen quick mentions on several blogs about cooking them in a Crock-Pot. To my surprise, the Butterball brand of turkey roast I bought had instructions on the side. True to my nature, I had to "improve" those instructions to come up with my own version.

Set a 4-quart Crock-Pot near the sink. Not plugged in yet, you just need the Crock right by the sink at this point. Remove the plastic wrapper from a 3-pound turkey breast roast (Butterball is great, but any brand should work). Leave the string "net" over the roast intact. Put the breast roast into the Crock with the fatty portion side up.

Rinse all juices out of the plastic wrappings and toss in garbage can without scattering raw chicken juice all over the floor or counters. Using soap, vigorously wash hands; also wash gravy packet if one was included in the roast package.

With clean, dry hands, pour approx. 1½ cups of apple juice into the Crock. I tend to use unsweetened apple juice, but regular apple juice would be good. Apple cider will kick the taste up another little bit, too. Sprinkle black pepper over turkey and a little down into the juice. A little dash or two of cayenne pepper will kick the taste a bit for those who like it spicy.

Place Crock back into the pot and cover; situate near an electrical outlet. Cook on low in Crock for at least 7 hours. It can easily take another 1–2 hours of low cooking if you've got one of those superlong days.

Once it has finished cooking, remove turkey roast from Crock and let sit on a plate for about 20 minutes to cool off before attempting to cut the string net off the meat. Caution: the meat is superhot at this stage. I've about burned off a few areas of my fingerprints because I don't like waiting long enough for it to cool.

While the roast is cooling, pour all the liquid and scrapings from the bottom of the Crock into a saucepan to make gravy. If your turkey had a gravy packet with it, add that packet to the liquid and scrapings in the saucepan. I do have to add some thickener (I use arrowroot powder) to get the gravy to thicken once it has warmed up, mostly because my back gets tired quickly when I'm standing at the stove for that long.

Once turkey has been freed from its string net and the gravy is at the consistency you prefer, serve up and enjoy!

Punch Bowl Cake

Submitted by Wanda Downs

1 box yellow cake mix
2 (5 oz.) pkgs. instant vanilla pudding mix
5 cups milk
6 bananas
2 (21 oz.) cans cherry pie filling
2 (20 oz.) cans crushed pineapple, drained
6 oz. coconut
1(16 oz.) pkg. frozen whipped topping, thawed
¼ cup chopped nuts (any kind)

Bake cake according to package directions for two-layer cake; let cakes cool.

Prepare pudding according to package with the 5 cups milk listed.

In a large punchbowl, start with one layer of the cake and break into pieces; spread with ½ of the pudding mix, then slice three bananas over the pudding and then layer one can drained pineapple, one can pie filling, and half of the coconut.

Repeat in the same order with the remaining ingredients.

Top with whipped cream, then sprinkle with nuts, chill, then serve.

Peanut Butter Cookies

Submitted by Elaine Robinson

I have won awards for these cookies at the Barnstable County Fair in July, but Christmas without these cookies just doesn't seem quite right. I work as a nurse in a nursing home, and over the years, I have given these cookies as gifts to staff. At one of the nursing homes I worked at in the past, the woman who took care of the staff scheduling would request these cookies from time to time. Of course I complied and baked her a plate, and jokingly stated I wanted my vacation time!

1 cup peanut butter
¼ cup butter
1 egg
½ white sugar
½ brown sugar
1 tsp. vanilla
1 cup flour

Preheat oven to 350 degrees.

Mix peanut butter, butter, and egg; add sugars and vanilla. Mix in flour, adding more if necessary. Roll dough between hands and flatten, placing on cookie sheet. Cookie sheet can be greased, or use aluminum foil.

Cook for 10 minutes; oven times may vary.

When cookies are removed from oven, an extra treat is to place a Hershey Kiss on top of each cookie.

Mexican Wedding Bells

Submitted by Pam Curran

This recipe is from my mother, Alva Wheeler. I have been making it for years and it is a tradition, especially at Christmas.

1 cup butter (½ cup margarine, ½ cup shortening)
6 tbs. confectioner's sugar (powdered)
2 cups flour
1 tsp. vanilla
1 cup chopped pecans

Cream butter and sugar. Add flour, vanilla, and pecans. Spoon by
tablespoon onto ungreased cookie sheet and bake for 20 minutes in a 350-degree preheated oven.

When cool, cover with confectioner's sugar until well

coated. I put mine into a paper sack and shake until covered with sugar.

These cookies freeze well.

Santa Whiskers

Submitted by Nancy Farris

These cookies have been a Farris family staple at Christmas. It just wouldn't be the holidays without them.

1 cup butter, softened
1 cup sugar
2 tbs. milk
1 tsp. vanilla extract
2½ cup flour
¾ cup total of finely chopped red and green candied cherries
½ cup finely chopped pecans
⅓ cup flaked coconut

In a mixer bowl, cream together butter and sugar. Blend in milk and vanilla. Stir in flour, cherries, and pecans. Form into two logs, each 2" in diameter and 8" long. Roll each log in coconut, pressing lightly to make it stick. Wrap each log in plastic wrap and chill for several hours or overnight.

Heat oven to 375 degrees. Slice into ¼" slices and place on greased cookie sheet. Bake for 12 minutes or until edges are golden.

Almond Banket (Amandel Staaf, **Dutch Holiday Pastry)**

Submitted by Joanne Kocourek

A banket is a traditional Dutch Christmas dessert often given as a gift. Dutch families produce the "letters" as well as BANKET (sticks) in celebration of Christmas and special occasions. The custom of edible letters goes back to Germanic times, when children were given an A, made of bread, as a symbol of good fortune. During the 16th and 17th centuries pastry letters were captured in Dutch Masters' still-life paintings.

Pastry:

1 lb. *cold* butter (It needs to be cold, and cut into smaller chunks, so that it breaks into grainy granules, rather than just creaming into the flour)
4 cups flour
½ tsp. salt
1 cup ice water

If using a food processor, mix the butter, flour, and salt first, then drizzle in the ice water a little at a time, *just* until the dough forms a ball. (It might be a little less or a little more than 1 cup, and it *must* be ice water.) If mixing by hand, cut the butter into the dry ingredients with a pastry cutter until all the butter is mixed in and the mixture is grainy. Then add the water a little at a time. Chill overnight.

Filling:

1 lb. almond paste, crumbled (don't use marzipan; it has to be almond paste)
2 cup granulated sugar
2 eggs
Optional: 1 tsp. almond extract or 2 tbs. Grand Marnier or amaretto liqueur

Mix completely. Chill overnight.

Topping:

In a small bowl, whisk 2 eggs with ¼ cup water.
Slivered almonds or granulated sugar (optional)

Divide filling into 10–12 equal parts. Cut dough into 10–12 equal parts. Take one part and roll into a long strip (around 15-12″ long and about 6″ wide). Put one portion of the filling along the strip in the middle, making an even ridge of filling about 1/2″ wide. Leave 1″ of dough free on the ends. Fold the ends of the dough over the filling. Fold one side up over the filling, then the other. Using a pastry brush, brush egg/water mixture along the seams and use fingers to seal.

Place tube (it will be around 1–2″ in diameter) on a long cookie sheet, seam side down. Brush top with egg/water mixture and sprinkle with a little sugar and/or almond slivers. Repeat procedure with each of the 10–12 dough/filling portions. (I usually bake 5–6 sticks on a cookie sheet.) Pierce the tops every 2–4 inches with a fork. Bake in 375 to 400 degree oven for 30 to 35 minutes, until the top of the pastry is golden brown. Bake one pan at a time.

Don't be alarmed if some of the almond paste spills out; it is a favorite sneaky snack in our house to eat the spilled almond paste after the pans come out of the oven.

Let the pastry cool completely, then wrap tightly in plastic wrap. To serve, cut in 1–2″ slices.

Festive Fudge

Submitted by Kathleen J. Kaminski

Making this Festive Fudge has become a Christmas tradition for me. While I love Christmas cookies, I generally don't have the time to make them; instead, I make this fudge, to eat myself and also to give as presents! I generally make three kinds—with nuts, with marshmallow, and a chocolate mint. For the chocolate mint I use mint chocolate chips instead of regular (you can also mix part mint with regular for a lighter mint taste). Then I crush up some candy canes and sprinkle that on top before cooling. I got the recipe from my mom.

3 cups (18 oz.) semisweet chocolate chips (or milk chocolate chips)
1 (14 oz.) can sweetened condensed milk (*not* evaporated milk)
Dash of salt
½–1 cup chopped nuts (optional)
1½ tsp. vanilla extract

In heavy saucepan, over low heat, melt chips with condensed milk and salt (or microwave). Remove from heat, stir, and add vanilla. Spread evenly into wax paper–lined 8- or 9-in. square pan.

Chill two hours or until firm. Turn fudge onto cutting board, peel off paper, and cut into squares.

Store covered in refrigerator.

Marshmallow fudge:

Proceed as above but omit nuts and add 2 tbs. butter to mixture. Fold in 2 cups miniature marshmallows.

I've done other variations as well: using mint chocolate chips instead of or mixed with the regular chocolate chips, then sprinkling crushed candy canes on top of the evenly spread mix, using some raspberry-flavored chocolate chips, etc.

Peanut Brittle

Submitted by Vivian Shane

This recipe is an oldie but goodie; it was given to me by my mother. My cooking style tends toward simple types of recipes and this one is relatively easy. The result is much tastier than the commercial type of brittle!

2 cups sugar
1 cup light corn syrup
½ cup water
1 cup (2 sticks) butter
2 cups salted peanuts
1 tsp. soda

Heat and stir sugar, syrup, and water in a heavy 3-quart saucepan until sugar dissolves. Continue to cook and stir until syrup boils, blends in butter. Cook, stirring occasionally, to 230 degrees on candy thermometer. Stir often after temperature reaches 230, and continue to cook to 280, then add peanuts. Stir constantly to 305 (hard crack stage). Remove from heat and quickly stir in soda, mixing well. Pour into buttered cookie sheet. Remove from pan as soon as candy is set and break into pieces. Store in tightly covered container. Makes 2¼ lbs.

Divinity

Submitted by Pam Curran

This one came from a very special aunt who was like my second mother, who used to bake a lot and make candy. She made pies to sell to our local cafés. I wish I had some of her pie recipes. This was always a must-have around the holidays for us.

3 cups sugar
1 cup Karo white syrup
½ cup water
¼ tsp. salt
2 egg whites
1 tsp. vanilla
1 cup pecans
Cherries (if desired)

Cook sugar, Karo, water, and salt until it cracks in cold water (hard boil stage). Remove from heat. Beat (mixer) egg whites until stiff and gradually add syrup to them, beating constantly.
Continue beating until it loses its gloss and add vanilla, pecans, and cherries. Pour into buttered platter and cut into squares.

Yorkshire Pudding

Submitted by Janel Flynn

This recipe was my Grandmother Emerick's recipe. She used to make this at her bed-and-breakfast in Massachusetts with roast beef. Really good with gravy on top.

1 cup sifted flour
½ tsp. salt
1 cup milk
2 eggs, well beaten

Sift flour and salt together.

Gradually add milk and eggs, which you have combined. Beat until smooth.
Pour into pan that has about ¼ cup hot drippings from a roast beef.

Bake in hot oven at 450 degrees for 25–30 minutes or until golden brown.

Serve with roast beef and gravy.

Books by Kathi Daley

Come for the murder, stay for the romance.

Buy them on Amazon today.

Zoe Donovan Cozy Mystery:

Halloween Hijinks
The Trouble With Turkeys
Christmas Crazy
Cupid's Curse
Big Bunny Bump-off
Beach Blanket Barbie
Maui Madness
Derby Divas
Haunted Hamlet
Turkeys, Tuxes, and Tabbies
Christmas Cozy
Alaskan Alliance
Matrimony Meltdown
Soul Surrender
Heavenly Honeymoon
Hopscotch Homicide
Ghostly Graveyard
Santa Sleuth
Shamrock Shenanigans – *January 2016*

Paradise Lake Cozy Mystery:

Pumpkins in Paradise
Snowmen in Paradise
Bikinis in Paradise
Christmas in Paradise
Puppies in Paradise
Halloween in Paradise

Whales and Tails Cozy Mystery:

Romeow and Juliet
The Mad Catter
Grimm's Furry Tail
Much Ado About Felines
Legend of Tabby Hollow
Cat of Christmas Past
A Tale of Two Tabbies – *February 2016*

Seacliff High Mystery:

The Secret
The Curse
The Relic
The Conspiracy
The Grudge – *December 2015*

Road to Christmas Romance:

Road to Christmas Past

Kathi Daley lives with her husband, kids, grandkids, and Bernese mountain dogs in beautiful Lake Tahoe. When she isn't writing, she likes to read (preferably at the beach or by the fire), cook (preferably something with chocolate or cheese), and garden (planting and planning, not weeding). She also enjoys spending time on the water when she's not hiking, biking, or snowshoeing the miles of desolate trails surrounding her home.

Kathi uses the mountain setting in which she lives, along with the animals (wild and domestic) that share her home, as inspiration for her cozy mysteries.

Stay up-to-date with her newsletter, *The Daley Weekly*. There's a link to sign up on both her Facebook page and her website, or you can access the sign-in sheet at: http://eepurl.com/NRPDf

Visit Kathi:

Facebook at Kathi Daley Books, **www.facebook.com/kathidaleybooks**

Kathi Daley Teen – **www.facebook.com/kathidaleyteen**

Kathi Daley Books Group Page – **https://www.facebook.com/groups/569578823146850/**

Kathi Daley Books Birthday Club- get a book on your birthday - https://www.facebook.com/groups/1040638412628912/

Kathi Daley Recipe Exchange - https://www.facebook.com/groups/752806778126428/

Webpage - www.kathidaley.com

E-mail - kathidaley@kathidaley.com

Recipe Submission E-mail – kathidaleyrecipes@kathidaley.com

Goodreads: https://www.goodreads.com/author/show/7278377.Kathi_Daley

Twitter at Kathi Daley@kathidaley - https://twitter.com/kathidaley

Tumblr - http://kathidaleybooks.tumblr.com/

Amazon Author Page - http://www.amazon.com/Kathi-Daley/e/B00F3BOX4K/ref=sr_tc_2_0?qid=1418237358&sr=8-2-ent

Pinterest - http://www.pinterest.com/kathidaley/

Made in the USA
Middletown, DE
08 December 2015